RACHEL ANDERSON

— The —
Bus People

Henry Holt and Company • New York

Henry Holt and Company, Inc.
Publishers since 1866
115 West 18th Street
New York, New York 10011

Henry Holt is a registered
trademark of Henry Holt and Company, Inc.

Copyright © 1989 by Rachel Anderson
All rights reserved.
First published in the United States in 1992
by Henry Holt and Company, Inc.
Published in Canada by Fitzhenry & Whiteside Ltd.,
195 Allstate Parkway, Markham, Ontario L3R 4T8.
Originally published in Great Britain in 1989
by Oxford University Press.

Library of Congress Cataloging-in-Publication Data
Anderson, Rachel.
    The bus people. Rachel Anderson.
Summary: The lives of the passengers on Bertram's
"fruit-cake bus" are shaped by the experiences and problems
each has faced because of different disabilities.
[1. Handicapped—Fiction.   2. School buses—Fiction
3. England—Fiction.]   I. Title.
PZ7.A5489Bu   1992   [Fic]—dc20   92-1506

ISBN 0-8050-2297-X (hardcover)
10 9 8 7 6 5 4 3
ISBN 0-8050-4250-4 (paperback)
10 9 8 7 6 5 4 3 2 1

First American hardcover edition published in 1989
by Henry Holt and Company, Inc.
First American paperback edition, 1995

Printed in the United States of America
on acid-free paper. ∞

To Nicola Kane

·CONTENTS·

— The —
BusPeople

1

BERTRAM
IN THE MORNING

*T*he mini-bus is driven by Bertram. It's licensed to carry thirteen passengers, though there'll only be seven on board today. Bertram collects his passengers at the start of their day. Bertram takes them home again, right to their own front doors, at the end of the afternoon.

Bertram wears his old blue donkey jacket, and carries an unlit cigarette between his lips. The government's warnings about lung cancer don't bother Bertram. When you've been driving the fruit-cake bus as long as him, you've seen more of life and so you're not afraid of a painful death. That's what Bertram says anyhow.

He'll light up as soon as he gets to Andy's house. There's always a bit of a wait for Andy to come out.

Bertram reverses out of the parking bay, backs round the locked petrol pumps, slides narrowly past the other buses, and across the yard. The cold engine coughs. Bertram's flaccid lungs cough. Bertram isn't a fit man, not A1. That's why they put him on the fruit-cake run.

"You'll take the specials, O.K., Bert?" the boss told him. That was three years back when he'd just come out of the hospital. Lung trouble. The boss wanted Bertram to have it easy.

" 'Fraid it's a bit of an early start on the specials. But any rate you'll get a nice quiet day to yourself. Till you go to pick 'em up again at three."

"Right on," said Bertram to his boss. "Special run it is."

Bertram's been doing it ever since. He's come to really love his fruit-cake run. You get to know your passengers, Bertram says, when you see them every day. Bertram likes the early start.

"Then you know you're alive, don't you?" he says. "Get the roads to yourself too."

So here we are, ten past seven in the morning, and he's already swinging out onto the road while all over town most normal citizens and clerks and school-kids are still crawling out from between the sheets, groping towards their bathroom mirrors to check who they are, grappling with their boiled eggs, fighting with their shoelaces.

But not Bertram's crew. They'll all be ready for him when he calls by, all except for Andy, that is.

"A rum lot, my team," said Bertram. "Nutty as fruit-cakes, most of them. That's why I get on so well with them." And he laughs. "I like 'em that way. Wouldn't swap my fruit-cakes for the world." Which is just as well, because none of the other drivers ever seem to want to have a crack at the fruit-cake run. What with the fits, and the shrieks, the nodding heads, and the rolling eyes.

Here he comes now, swerving round the roundabout, down Iris Avenue, across Tudor Terrace, and into Jubilee Gardens to pick up Andy.

Bertram sounds the horn outside Andy's house, letting Andy's dad, as well as the rest of the silent street, know he's there. Andy's dad already knows. Andy's chair is ready standing out on the pavement. Bertram loads it onto the bus and climbs back into his driver's seat. Time to light up and relax while he waits for Andy. There's never any point in getting impatient with any of his crew.

In Andy's house, there's a lot of scuffling going on. Andy's the eldest of four.

Let trumpets sound and carrillons play! For here comes Andy now, triumphant, ready to face the day, down the garden path, cradled in his father's arms, tiny king of his family, worshipped and adored. With three doting sisters and two loving parents, Andy need never lift a finger. Andy can't ever lift a finger.

Andy's father is in his bathrobe. There's never time to dress till the king of the roost has been seen on his way.

"Wotcha there, matey!" Bertram calls through the driver's window.

But Andy doesn't reply, for he must concentrate with all the might of his frail hands on clinging to the broad terry-toweling of his father's shoulder.

Andy's in, seat belt securely strapped, just in case of accidents. Bertram has never had an accident in thirty years behind the wheel. But just supposing he did, with this precious royal cargo on board?

"Croak, croak," says Andy.

"See the match last night?" Bertram asks.

Andy raises his withered hand and nods. "Croak, croak," he says.

"His tablets, Bertram. In his pocket. Tell Mrs. Lovegrove." Through the driver's window which is closed, Andy's father mimes tablets, pockets, and swallowing. Bertram nods and waves. Message received. Over and out, and on our way.

Mrs. Lovegrove is the escort lady. Bertram goes to her house straight after Andy's. According to the terms of the vehicle insurance, according to the rules of the bus company, according to the local authority education laws, Bertram may not take on board a single passenger until the escort is there, ready to cope in case of incidents.

"But it seems daft, doesn't it, doing it that way round,"

3

says Bertram, "when Mrs. Lovegrove lives just beyond Andy's home. I'd have to go all the way up Jubilee Gardens right past his house to fetch Mrs. L. And then all the way right down again. No sense in that, is there?"

Mrs. Lovegrove agrees. So she and Bertram carry on doing things their way, making up their own rules, ignoring the ones thought up by other men and women in suits in official departments.

"Bye, Cinderella!" Bertram waves to Andy's sister, standing on the doorstep in her nightie. "Have a good day."

"Croak, croak," says the king, who likes to be alone in Bertram's bus, as though it were all his own, as though he were making a morning tour of his domain. Up Jubilee Gardens, down Coronation Grove. Pity it's not further to Mrs. Lovegrove's. Though any distance is far enough to have a seizure. And what would happen then? How would Bertram cope? How would he drive the bus *and* see to his passenger's royal tongue and regal lolling head? Let's not count our problems before they've happened, thinks Bertram. Andy won't go having no seizures, not here on my bus, even if Marilyn sometimes does.

"We're all right, then, aren't we, me old matey?" Bertram half-turns to say to Andy.

Yes, I'm all right, thinks the king, seated behind his chauffeur, tied onto his throne, smiling and waving at the chirping sparrows in the privet hedges of his domain.

"D'you know, sometimes I think our Andy's one of the happiest kids alive," said Andy's father once to Andy's mother.

Bertram would agree with that. And so would Andy.

So now we've got Bertram and Andy. Then in half a moment, there'll be Mrs. Lovegrove, and Rebecca, and surly Micky who never speaks. Who are the others who, day by day, month by month, travel on Bertram's fruitcake bus?

2

REBECCA

*O*n Friday afternoon, Rebecca, plump and pretty in green, scrambled to reach the door of the school bus the moment it stopped. Usually she moved slowly and thoughtfully. But today she was down the steps, across the gravel, and struggling with the latch of the front gates well before Mrs. Lovegrove, the bus escort, had time to get up and help her.

"Hey, Beccy! Beccy! Your bag! You've left your bag!" Mrs. Lovegrove shook it like a duster out of the bus door.

Rebecca went back reluctantly.

"And what's all the rush for, anyway?"

"It's her sister," said Bertram, who usually knew everything about everybody, for he read the *City Gazette* with care, spotting familiar names, faces, forthcoming events.

"Wedding," Rebecca agreed.

"Gonna be a right fair do, ain't it? Champagne, cake, music, six bridesmaids. And it's our Madam Beccy here what's gonna be the belle of the ball, ain't you, ducks? Sister to the bride, so that makes her chief bridesmaid. Blue, didn't you say?"

Rebecca shook her head in despair at Bertram's poor

memory for detail. She had been discussing wedding plans with him ever since her sister's engagement was first announced. She knew she had described to him at least twice the color of the bridesmaids' dresses. How could he forget?

"No to *blue*, Bertram. Never mind. I tell you again. It's pink, pinky, pink. And I tell you before, lots of times."

Tomorrow was the happy day, the most beautiful day since Rebecca's life began fifteen years ago in the labor ward. As chief bridesmaid, she had the third most important job of the day. The most important went to Jane, as bride. The second most important went to Graham who was to marry Jane.

"Bertram, I show you pictures after," said Rebecca kindly and she climbed back up the steps of the bus to give him a hug. Too late, she remembered her mother's constant reminder that she was not to show physical affection to any person who was not part of her family.

"D'you understand me, darling? Now you're a big girl, you have to stop hugging people you don't know, especially men."

The introduction of yet another rule of conduct dated back to a day when Rebecca was feeling particularly friendly towards the butcher, in his blood-stained apron. Instead of staring at her before turning quickly away as most people did when they saw her coming, he'd waved at her over the lamb chops.

"Why?" said Rebecca, in surprise.

"Because," said her mother vaguely. "Just because. It isn't the done thing. You never know where a hug can lead. Specially with a girl like you."

Rebecca knew exactly what *that* meant. It meant a girl with 47 chromosomes instead of 46 for, unlike sulky Micky on the bus, who often didn't know what he was or why he was, Rebecca was quite clear on these matters. Her mother had told her from the start precisely where she stood.

"You are a Down's Syndrome sufferer. It's not your fault. But it means you'll never be the same as your sister Jane, nor the rest of us."

Her father, more gently, had said, "But it doesn't matter who a person is, or what a person looks like, so long as a person is loved. And you, Rebecca, are loved."

When, some weeks later, Rebecca had inadvertently hugged the milkman as he set down a carton of orange juice and a natural yoghurt four-pack, her mother reminded her once again of the social behavior appropriate to people with that extra chromosome.

"We do not show physical affection to grown men!" she said sharply.

"Not even my Bertram?" said Rebecca, petulant. She spent more hours of her life in the company of Bertram, sitting on the bus, watching the back of his neck than she spent with any other adult male, including her father. Bertram was her best friend.

"No. Quite definitely not Bertram. I've just explained it to you, but I will explain again. You are not to embrace any men, however nice they seem. I shall have to have a word with that driver about it."

"Not even *Daddy?*" Rebecca asked, checking her mother for consistency.

"Of *course* you can hug Daddy. He's your father. That's different."

"And Jamie? Not Jamie?"

Jamie was a cousin whom Rebecca was allowed occasionally to hold on her lap. Jamie was two years old and did not yet know about Rebecca's extra chromosome nor that, because of the chromosome, she was considered by some to be a species apart.

"Of course you can still hug Jamie. He's your first cousin. He's part of our family."

Gradually, by a process of trial and error but mostly error, Rebecca learned her mother's rules of etiquette. Her father seemed less concerned and continued, whenever he was around, to give Rebecca boisterous bear hugs which squeezed the air out of her, making her gasp and giggle at the same time.

"Now, missy! Steady on there!" said Bertram who'd known all the rules of hugging long before Rebecca's mother ever explained them to him. "Don't go wearing yourself out, or you'll have no energy left to hold your sister's bouquet." He released himself from Rebecca's grasp and gave her a pat on the shoulder. "Have a great day now!"

"Bye bye bye!" Rebecca waved to Bertram, to Mrs. Lovegrove, and to those of her travelling companions whose faces, still pressed to the bus windows, were apparently looking out. But Micky, Darryl, Andy and Marilyn, every day, twice a day, spring, summer, autumn, and winter for years and years, had seen the driveway leading up to Rebecca's gracious home. So now, they merely stared out with glazed unseeing eyes.

And in so doing, they missed a surprising change in the view. Rising steadily, inch by inch, above the high clipped hedges which surrounded the house, appeared a giant wedding cake, white with red wooden bobbles on the top. Rebecca wondered for a moment what it was, then realized, with excitement, that the wedding had begun.

Jane had told her that things would seem a bit strange this weekend. This must be what she'd meant.

"Bye bye bye!" Rebecca sang as she raced up the drive on her tiny fat flat feet, surprisingly graceful for 144 pounds and 4 feet 9 inches tall, round the hedge, along the herbaceous borders where the lazy afternoon bees hummed among the lavender, to the lawn beneath the drawing room windows where seven hairy men were straining on ropes, hauling up the canvas, to make a huge white tent stand up like a hollow cake with scarlet icing on top, all for the great and happy day.

But these seven loud men in overalls were, Rebecca knew, no part of the family. Much as she longed to stay and watch, she knew that rules were rules. She must ignore the exciting progress of the marquee's steady rise. Somehow, she must pretend it wasn't there. Nor the seven noisy men shouting and calling to each other and making holes in her father's smooth green lawns with their pegs and hammers and feet.

Rebecca went indoors, headed straight for the kitchen, and sat down at the table to wait, as she did on normal days, for her mother to prepare the tea. Curiously, today no tea cups, teapot, milk or spoons had been laid. Nor did her mother appear, though Rebecca could plainly hear her voice elsewhere in the house. In fact, she could hear many people in the house. Everything was disturbingly topsy-turvy. But Rebecca would not let herself be upset. Her sister had told her it might be like this.

"You love me, don't you, Beccy?" Jane had said. "So you'll put up with all the turmoil of a wedding day, won't you darling? Just for my sake?"

Rebecca had nodded. An important request asked in a solemn moment together. Her sister was good. Her sister had asked *her* to be chief bridesmaid. "Beccy darling, you do see that after the wedding, nothing will ever be quite the same. But you know how much I love Graham, don't you, and how I want to be with him always?"

Yes, Rebecca knew. She knew it meant that Jane wouldn't be living here, ready to love and protect Rebecca as she had always done before. But Rebecca knew that Jane's love for Graham was as important as Rebecca's love for Jane.

"I got forty-seven chromosomes," she told her sister, as though Jane did not already know. "You got forty-six. You marry Graham. You got new white dress. I got new pinky."

Through the kitchen window she watched the men at work, though she did not let them see her watching. Weddings, Rebecca knew, meant disorder as well as happiness, for Jane had told her so.

"But it'll only be chaotic for the one weekend. Then you'll all be back to normal again."

"Normal again," agreed Rebecca. "All just the same."

"Well, no, not *exactly* the same of course," said Jane. "Because after I'm married, I'll be living with Graham."

"Living with Graham who loves you."

"That's it. Gosh, by then I'll be a Mrs. Isn't that extraordinary? I can hardly believe it."

"Then not living here, not any more."

"That's right, darling. I won't be here because I'll be moving to the new flat. Remember you came and saw it when I was making the curtains?"

Yes, Rebecca remembered.

"But you'll come and stay with us lots and lots. And then after a bit I'll have babies. Well, I hope I'll have babies because that's what we both want. And you'll come and stay and you'll be their aunt. Won't that be terrific?"

"Aunt," said Rebecca. "Why aunt?"

"Because that's just the way it works, doesn't it? If I have children, you'll be an aunt. But before that, you'll be a bridesmaid and get a present. Each of the bridesmaids do. Graham's chosen them. A pearl necklace for you, because you're nearly grown up, and silver brooches for the little girls."

The marquee, its topmost ridge now on a level with the bedroom windows, made Rebecca think of a great white ark waiting to be filled with creatures arriving, two by two, and all in their pairs. The lion and the lioness. The ram and the ewe. The stallion and the mare.

Tomorrow Rebecca would be wearing the dress of oyster-pink taffetta with its gathered sleeves and long full skirts, and she would be there to hold her sister's bouquet while her sister's fiancé put the golden ring on Jane's marriage finger. And then, before they walked back down the church as man and wife, she would return the bouquet of roses, lilies and dainty white bows for her sister to carry. As they came out of the church for the photographs, Rebecca would be there just behind them, and behind her would be the little bridesmaids. By tomorrow, Jane would be a wife and this great white ark would be filled with its people.

Three of the workmen in overalls came into the kitchen carrying a roll of artificial grass.

"Your mum around, love?" one asked Rebecca.

With his bushy eyebrows, he looked, Rebecca thought, almost like her father. But of course she knew that he wasn't. So she said nothing. She knew she must not talk to strangers. She must never talk to strangers, even if they tried to speak to her. She must never talk to men she did not know.

"Never mind, duckie," said the man. " 'Spect I can find her myself if I look."

Until the men had gone from the kitchen, Rebecca kept her eyes turned downwards and gazed at her hands, whose shape was better known to her even than her own face. Despite the chaos in the house, she knew she was safe because she was a loved child. Her father had told her so. Being loved was the most important thing in the world.

When people laughed and called you a dummy dumbo, it didn't hurt if you knew that at home in the family there were always people who loved you.

Although she waited quietly and patiently, her mother still did not come to give Rebecca her tea. So Rebecca made her way cautiously through the house, following the sound of her mother's voice.

The hall was stacked with brown cartons. Rebecca knew she must not touch anything which was not hers for when she touched things, sometimes they broke. But without touching too much, she nudged up the lids of the cartons and looked in at the fragile stemmed glasses and the green and gold champagne bottles. More strangers hurried through the hall and began carrying the cartons through to the marquee.

Standing in the hall, Rebecca heard her mother's voice drifting from the drawing room. There were several other women in there. And Rebecca could hear the clink of cups too. They were drinking tea. She was surprised that her mother should have started tea without waiting for her. So she stayed outside the drawing room door.

"Barbara darling, I think the moment's come." One of the women spoke with a voice which sounded almost like her mother's, yet was not her mother. It was more brittle than her mother's. "The moment she gets in from whatever that place is she goes to."

"It's a school, a special school," said Rebecca's mother's voice slowly. "Yes, I suppose you're right. Though I don't know *how* I'm to put it to her. She's been so looking forward to it all. Almost more than anybody. Specially the dress. We've had two fittings with the dressmaker."

"It must be said. No good waiting and waiting till the very last moment," said the brittle woman.

"Jane won't be pleased either," said Rebecca's mother's voice. "They're very close, those two. You'd be surprised."

"Strange, isn't it, when they're so different?"

"Oh dear. It really is going to be so hard. Couldn't one of *you* say something?"

"Why us, for goodness' sake, my dear?"

"Because it just might seem easier for her coming from one of her aunts than from her mother."

Although Rebecca heard the words, she knew she must not allow herself to try to understand their meaning because, as her mother so often told her, girls like her were not always very good at understanding things and Rebecca often managed to misunderstand things which were actually quite simple.

So she returned to the kitchen, to sit quietly at the table watching her hands whose unchanging familiarity often gave reassurance in times of uncertainty.

She heard her sister's car pulling up on the drive, and her sister's terrier yapping as it was released and ran round in circles. She heard her mother hurrying across the gravel, and greeting Jane.

And once again, she heard the shrill women who were aunts. "It should've been the other way around, I always said. They should've called the mongol Jane, a plain Jane if ever there was one, and called the pretty one Rebecca."

The brittle words flowed like iced water out of the drawing room and along the corridor, and Rebecca knew that she must not let herself understand because then she would misunderstand.

"But there we are, they never did seem to see sense with that child, did they?"

"And now she's getting positively gross."

"They ought to have had her put away somewhere right from the start."

Rebecca knew she could only understand simple things, like her love for her sister, and her sister's love for Graham, and she could not, would not, understand difficult and important things like what the aunts' brittle words meant.

"Janie! Janie! Janie!" she cried with delight, jumping up and down in the kitchen and hugging her sister round the waist.

"Darling Beccy! Who's my very best sister, then? And did you know the aunts are here and so you're coming into my room for tonight? It's all so exciting isn't it? I told you it would be, didn't I? Shall we go and see what's going on in the garden? And then there's all those lovely presents upstairs to be sorted. Oh, and we must see how the flowers are coming on, mustn't we?"

There was so much to do.

Rebecca followed her sister as she made her busy bridal rounds.

"Gosh, Beccy darling. You're such a help! I don't know what I'd have done without you."

By evening, Rebecca was exhausted with the excitement.

"You won't want to have to sit through a long dinner party, will you dear?" said her mother. "Having to listen to all the grown ups talking? It'll be awfully dull for you."

Rebecca agreed that it might.

"So we thought you'd probably much prefer to have your supper early on a tray in front of the telly."

Rebecca felt quite relieved and agreed that she would. And after her supper in front of the television, she was keen to get upstairs to enjoy the rare treat of sharing a room with Jane. Her mother tucked her up in the camp bed at the foot of her sister's bed. Rebecca put herself to sleep thinking of her colors. Tomorrow would be a gold and pink sort of a day. Gold the sky, pink the roses. Pink the color of her sister's lips. Gold the color of her sister's hair. Gold the color of the sky. Gold the feeling of love in her heart. Pink the color of the bridesmaid dress.

The brittle voices woke her. Surrounded by the billows of tissue paper and the new clothes, and the dresses hanging in their plastic bags, Rebecca imagined at first that she was in a curious dream.

But the voices out on the landing were quite real. It was the aunts and her mother coming up after dinner.

"Now Ba, dear, we've been over this a dozen times. First thing in the morning, you must do it."

"This is supposed to be a family wedding. We don't want any embarrassments. You know it wouldn't be fair on poor Graham's family. Coming all this way. Now maybe if, despite the brain, she was something to look at, had a bit of grace about her, well that might be another matter."

Then Jane was up there too, angry.

"How dare you! How can you speak like this! He adores her. You all know that. I don't give a damn about what his family think. I'm marrying him, not all his relations. I thought you and Auntie Ella were supposed to be here to help. All you do is sit and meddle."

"Try and see it from her point of view, Jane dear. D'you suppose for a moment that *she* really wants to stand up there, in the middle of a packed church, and be stared at? It's for her own good. She can sit with cousin Roger. We'll make sure she's taken in well ahead of the crowds."

"Really, you're all being too awful! Anyone would think it was your wedding, not mine. Now, if you'll let me past, I must go down and walk the dog."

"Wedding nerves, poor lass. She'll see better by tomorrow."

"Talking, talking, talking," said Rebecca in the dark to her hands.

She woke early. Jane was sleeping with her dog curled

up on the bed beside her. Rebecca knew she must not wake them. Quietly, quietly as a mouse, she put on her dressing gown and went down to the kitchen to wait for the gold and pink day to begin. Outside, the great white ark glowed luminescent in the dawn, waiting for its cargo of couples.

Rebecca heard creaks on the stairs. Her father sometimes came down first and made a pot of tea when she could drink her tea sweetened with four spoonfuls of sugar, and sit close to him. Sometimes he hugged her till she squealed. Sometimes he said nothing. She was always safe.

But it was not her father. It was one of the aunts who sounded so like her mother but was not her mother.

Rebecca smiled. " 'Lo," she said. "Nice day for wedding."

The aunt glanced incuriously across at Rebecca as though she were a stopped clock, bared her teeth in a token smile and was gone. Rebecca could no longer pretend to herself she did not understand the meaning of yesterday's brittle stream of words.

Over breakfast, Rebecca's mother, trembling, announced to Rebecca the change in plans.

"So we've found a place for you to sit where you'll get a much better view. Near the back. Near the door where Jane comes in. You'll be the very first person to see her, before anybody else. All right then, darling?"

Rebecca nodded. She understood. She had understood all along. She had not misunderstood anything.

She understood that because she did not look like other girls of her age, because she was short and stout, because she had sparse lank hair, and small round hands, because she had begun her monthly bleeding at nine years old, because she had dry scaly skin patches, for all these reasons which could never be changed, she was not to wear the oyster-pink taffetta, was not to stand behind her sister in the church where God would see her, was not to lean forward at the correct moment, as practiced in the ponies' paddock with a bunch of buttercups. She understood quite clearly that because she had short stubby fingers with unusual fingerprint patterns on them, she was not to receive the bouquet from Jane at the moment just before Jane made her promises to love Graham for always. And because she, Rebecca, loved Jane more than anybody in the world, she would accept whatever the day offered.

"Yes," she said because she would never hurt her sister by crying. "And it's nice day for wedding."

"Oh, yes, it certainly is, dear. The weather forecast was really very good. Now listen carefully, there'll be a special pew reserved just for you and Roger. On the left hand side of the church."

"Roger?"

"Yes, darling. I've just been telling you. I knew you weren't listening properly. Roger, who's going to look after you and be your special friend all afternoon. When everyone else is busy. Aunty Vi's big boy."

"Aunty Vi."

"That's right. Her second son. You used to play together. Roger's your cousin. Rebecca, my dear, you must *try* and concentrate. There's going to be lots of relatives today and you've got to be as nice and polite as you possibly can to show them what a splendid girl you are."

Rebecca remembered Roger from a long time ago. There had been other children there too. Perhaps they had been cousins too. A rough game. She hadn't liked him then. He had got the others to roll her on the ground in the dead leaves. Then they had all run away. Roger had come back after the others had gone. That was all Rebecca could remember.

"Cousin."

17

"Yes, that's it. Well done, darling. Cousin Roger. And you'll get a *lovely* view of Jane as she comes into the church. You'll get the first view, before anyone else sees her. I expect she'll give you a special smile. And when she goes out again. And remember to keep your mouth shut or it'll show forever in all the photos. Oh dear, the caterers are going to be late. I'm sure they are. I just hope to goodness they haven't lost their way. The timing has to be just so. We don't want anything spoiling Jane's big day, do we now?"

Jane came down to breakfast in her honeymoon negligée and ate half a grapefruit.

"Lovely day for wedding, Jane," said Rebecca.

Jane said, "Listen, old bean. I'm ever so sorry about the bridesmaid's business. Really I am. But you'll still get the pearl necklace."

"Dun't matter." As her sister had already told her, a wedding wasn't merely about the day of getting married. It was about what happened afterwards. It was about love.

"Dun't matter, Jane," she repeated, in case her sister hadn't heard. "Not if I got you. And I got you. I happy. Today I going help you all day. Your best day today. And Graham best day. This most important day. Afterwards, everything different."

"Jane dear," said their mother. "You won't forget you're meant to be at the hairdresser's by ten, will you? So you better hurry along and get yourself dressed."

"I come help you," said Rebecca, getting up to go after her sister.

But her mother said, "No, Rebecca. Don't go pestering Jane just now, dear. She's got such a lot to get done. I know, why don't you take the dog for a walk round the garden?"

Before Jane was back from the hairdresser, Rebecca was helped into her navy corduroy smock, her black patent strap shoes, and a pair of clean white knee-socks. She never liked wearing white knee-socks. The elastic tops cut into her legs just below her knees. They were pink round knees on which she sometimes rested her chin when sitting in the bath. She did not like the tight elastic and she did not like her knees showing below her hem.

"Now, dear," said her mother as Rebecca tugged at the elastic tops. "Just be very sensible today, won't you? For Jane's sake."

Rebecca's hair was brushed, her face was washed and she was taken to the church and placed in the care of Aunt Vi's big boy, Roger.

Cousin Roger looked like a man now and wore a man's dark suit with a carnation in his button hole. He had a man's deep voice, and big man's hands with fine dark hairs growing on them.

"Hello, Rebecca," he boomed as he led her to their selected rear pew, nicely sheltered by a stone pillar and a floral mass arranged on a pedestal. "Remember me? Your beastly boy cousin? Hope I've improved a bit since then. I'm studying to be a vet at college. I'm going to look after horses when I qualify."

At first, the church was nearly empty, apart from the ushers and the flower arrangements. But as it filled up, two by two, Rebecca was able to watch the backs of the people's heads, and the backs of the ladies' hats, and the backs of the men's necks.

Then she heard the rustle of arrivals at the porch and the hush which rippled through the congregation and the singing of a hymn, How love was divine, and was all love excelling. She heard the tippy-tappy of five small bridesmaids coming pitter-patter down the aisle, to the sighs of admiration. And, from her special pew behind the pillar, behind the flowers, where she stood with her long-ago

19

cousin Roger, Rebecca could see nothing beyond the broad black shoulders of the man immediately in front. She could not see the bridesmaids. She could not see her parents. She could not see if her sister was remembering to give her that special smile.

But she heard the vicar's words, "God is love, and those who live in love live in God and God lives in them." Such things, she knew, she was not supposed to try to understand because she would be bound to misunderstand.

She wondered what Cousin Roger could see, what he could hear, what he understood. She wanted to reach out to touch his hand, to take hold of him and hug him tight as her father sometimes hugged her.

Then she heard the vicar speak of the holy mystery in which man and woman become one flesh, and she understood that, however much she wanted to, she must not touch Cousin Roger's hand, must not hug him, must never hug any man. She understood that because she had forty-seven chromosomes, she would never be like Jane and wear a bridal gown, never know the holy mysteries.

"To have and to hold," said the vicar's voice.

"To have and to hold," replied Jane's tiny voice. "To love and to cherish."

"Can't see!" Rebecca whispered to her cousin. "Can't see nothing nothing anything at all!"

She looked up at him and saw that he wasn't even trying to see over the heads to the front. Instead, he was staring down at her knees.

He laughed and patted her hand.

"Nor can I!" he said. "But your knees are positively amazing! I don't think I've ever seen any knees like yours before."

"We can't see nothing nothing at all, can we?" Rebecca giggled. "Except knees."

And they both laughed.

As the last of the guests drove away, Rebecca's mother, standing amongst the debris of the feast in the empty space of the marquee, took off her hat.

"Well, I think that went off all right, didn't it?" she said to Rebecca's father.

"Yes, indeed," said Rebecca's father. "Splendidly."

"And I think everybody enjoyed themselves, don't you? And everybody said Jane looked lovely. And Graham spoke up so well. And all the—ah, here we are, Rebecca dear. And you too." Rebecca's mother took Rebecca's hand, and tucked it into the crook of her elbow. "You were a good girl. Everybody thought you behaved wonderfully too."

"And the dress," said Rebecca.

"The dress?" said her mother. "Oh yes, your dress. The pink dress. Of course we'll keep it. We won't let anyone else wear it. It'll still be *your* dress. Maybe you can wear it at Christmas? That'd be nice, wouldn't it? To wear it on Christmas Day when Cousin Roger's here again."

"Cold," said Rebecca.

"You're cold, darling? Surely not. I expect it's just after all the wonderful excitement. But I'll fetch your cardigan if you like."

"No. Cold at Christmas."

"Yes, that's right. It's usually cold at Christmas. And warm in the summer. Like now."

"Cold in that dress," said Rebecca. "At Christmas when it snow."

"Oh yes, I see. Yes, perhaps it would be. You could wear it with a woolly over. Or a pretty shawl."

"Never never wear that dress," said Rebecca. "No more weddings." Now that she understood everything about weddings, there was nothing more to do but sit quietly watching her two hands with the evening sunlight falling on them.

3

MICKY

*E*arly each morning, there is a female slave who rouses me, who washes me, who oils my body, who dresses me. The slave prepares my food. The slave feeds me.

"Morning, Micky, love. Nice sleepies? Happy dreams?"

I dreamed of chocolate biscuits, and ice cream, though I want to dream of something else which I can't yet understand.

"Time for wakey-wakies now, there's a good lad."

She opens the curtains. There are blue bears and yellow stars on the curtains. I want something different which I haven't found. It is to do with the touch of flesh. The slave is a woman and she touches flesh. But it is more than that.

"Up you come. Tablet time, pet."

That's her now, the slave come to rouse me.

"Schoolday, sleepyhead. Can't have our little lie-in today."

Too brutally for a caring slave, the woman rouses the drowsy youth. So let us face some facts. There is no slave. I live with my mother. She loves me to suffocation. And this has always been the order of my day. I live imprisoned inside a cage for two from which the only escape is a bus ride to school in the morning and a bus ride home in the evening. She stifles me with her love.

She pulls back the bed covers and removes the leg splints. Each is molded to the shape of a leg and held in place by black velcro straps. I find the sight of those short twisty legs encased in splints disturbing. I am glad when the splints are off.

"Tablet time, pet."

A man desires a woman to call his own whom he may hold close to him. A hand to hold. I seek my own body-woman I can do what I want with behind closed curtains.

"Here we are, dear. Got your old mum to take care of you. Swallow it down nicely."

She presses to my lips the spoonful of jam. In the jam are white chalky particles of bitter grit. The four tablets, crushed to powder, are disguised in raspberry conserve. No one is fooled by the sweet sticky lubrication of jam. These tablets inhibit the onset of the *status epilepticus* when the world revolves with nauseous lights and sounds and I slide down into a state of continuous fitting from which even my slave cannot arouse me.

"There's my good boy. Down the hatch."

That's what dad used to say. Now she says it.

Status epilepticus deprives me of oxygen, turns me purple, causes further brain damage. When I was younger, some mornings, I grinned and firmly clenched my teeth like a barred gate, forbidding entry to the spoon.

"Come on, dear. Don't be difficult today or we'll be all behind."

Yet inside herself, she liked it when I resisted. When I made my boyish rebellion, pretending I did not want to take my medication, then it seemed as though there was communication between us. A battle of wills proves a relationship. For ten minutes she must leave me lying on the bed while the tablets and jam go down into my crooked system. She drinks her cup of milky tea standing by the window in her dressing gown, chatting about the coming day's events, the weather, what Mrs. Thingy across the way is doing, whether the bus will be late or early.

The sameness of each day's conversation provides order and stability. She provides her own answers to her questions about the day, the weather, the neighbor, and the bus schedule. Bertram is always on time, like an automaton. And Mrs. Thingy is always in position behind her lace curtain across the road so that she can watch me, when the bus arrives, being wheeled out like the victim of some gross accident, and she can ask herself what sin my mum committed to have landed herself with such a son as this.

I do not want my mum to talk about the weather, and Mrs. Thingy. I want to think about the curious new power I have between my legs. Two of my legs are short and feeble, requiring splints to hold them straight and firm. The third lower limb, once as small and helpless as the other pair, is growing in strength, taking on its own life of energy.

"Who's my wetty boy, then? Never mind. Mum'll clean you up, make you nice and sweet again."

I am on the bed while she removes the pajamas, the plastic pants, the disposable diaper. Dreams of bodies wilt and fade. She washes me, dries me, smears Johnson's baby oil into the creases, replaces the soiled garments with fresh.

"There we are, my lamb."

Next, she stands me up from the bed, and leans me against the wall so that she can pull up my trousers, and fasten the fly. There is velcro fastening here too. She pats me on the head.

"Clean shirt for a clean boy."

24

There is always the problem with dribbling so I must wear a clean sweatshirt every day. I do not sweat because I take no exercise. Right Guard is not for me.

"Nearly brekkies time. And what's a good baby going to have today?"

She places my hands round her waist for balance and tucks the upper garments into my trousers. She pulls down my clean sweatshirt. MAN CITY is now written across my chest. She bought it through her mail order catalogue. She spent a long time choosing it from the colored pictures.

"Arsenal?" she read aloud. "Everton? Nottingham Forest?"

What did she mean?

"Which one d'you want to support, pet?"

When she had chosen the right wording she filled in the boxes in the order form and sent it off. I am glad she chose for me MAN CITY. But what does it mean? Who is MAN CITY? I did not attempt to ask her the meaning of the message, because she rarely tells me those things which she believes I do not need to know.

"Don't you go bothering your little head about all that, pet. You just let your old mum take care of the difficult things."

As soon as MAN CITY is on, she grasps my hands in hers and we move from the room. She walks backwards, I forwards, like an elegantly dancing couple, one step, two step, slip step, slow step, along the landing, down the stairs. She should have been re-housed years ago. Dad used to carry me down over one shoulder. Men are stronger than women.

Weetabix, bran-flakes, and prunes in syrup are ready on the table. Constipation is the scourge of the crumpled torso. My constipation causes her more trouble than it does me. The record is five days, after which point she calls in the

25

health visitor and the nurse who covers the bed in green rubber sheeting. Then it is enema time. Yee hah. Fun!

She flirts the spoon against my lips. My lips are closed. I neither like nor dislike prunes. But on principle I must refuse the first mouthful. Only when she has coaxed me enough, I part my lips and accept. In the end, I have no choice. I am enslaved to her care. My refusal is but a small step in the ritual dance into which we are both now locked.

Some people call her a saint. Year by year, she taught me to sit, to be quiet. That way, people liked me, or did not mind me.

"He's a bonny little chap, isn't it?" they said if I was still and silent, sitting like an egg in my wheelchair.

"Poor Mary. Fancy being left with a child like that," they said when I beat my head on the back of the chair, growled in my throat, dribbled, and roared, before finally slipping into the oblivion of *status epilepticus*.

Dad left years ago. It was the continual strain of living with her. But that was no way out for me, so I withdrew instead behind the blue bears and yellow stars which is where she wanted me. But now the expectation of more ice cream or an extra chocolate biscuit are no longer enough.

"There's the bus now, poppet. All ready, are we? On with your nice cozy jacket."

And then, in the schoolyard as I was being lifted from the bus, I heard the bus escort speaking and I learned that there was another possibility available to me. I discovered that I could move on from blue bears into another world.

"If only he was in the right place," said Mrs. Lovegrove. "He's so dependent on that mother of his. He could surely do more for himself."

I overheard the teacher to whom she was speaking say, "What about St. John Chrysostom's College for the Disabled?" And later they even tried to tell me about it, about how boys could live there during the term, sleep the nights there, not one night but many, so that, by day, they could learn the skills to help them become men and live in the world as men.

So a visit was arranged. When she heard about it, my mum didn't want to go.

"All that long way? I'd never manage the trains," she said.

She didn't want me to go either.

"He's doing ever so well as he is. He likes it in Mrs. Richards' group, don't you, pet?" When she calls me pet, she bends over and ruffles my hair. She stands behind me where I cannot see her face, and I imagine the milky pale hand of a hired woman from the market place caressing my ears and ruffling my hair.

"He'll have to leave special school eventually. It's as well to start looking around now."

"I wouldn't want him far off. He needs me."

They wondered at school what was planned for me when my mum grew old.

"He'll be stopping at home with me just so long as I can manage. I've always promised him that, and whatever you experts say to the contrary, I'm not going back on my word to him. If you have a boy like my Michael, he's got to have a lot more love than your ordinary kid. Some of you people don't seem to understand that. I'm sorry to speak my mind like this. But that's just how it is."

However, she was persuaded that there was nothing to lose by going to look at St. John Chrysostom's. We travelled by Local Authority taxi, me and my mum. Mrs. Lovegrove from the bus came too, as escort. Mrs. Lovegrove told my mum what a fine place St. John Chrysostom's was. I didn't need to listen. I already guessed in my flesh that it would be just the place for me, away from raspberry jam and curtains with pastel bears.

It was a large house, in a park, with big trees. As soon as we arrived they separated us, me from my mum. I could not believe my luck. I had been there no more than five minutes and already I had gained my first hold on freedom.

My mum was led off for coffee and an interview with the principal while I was taken over by a ginger-bearded man in his shirt sleeves. He was a teacher but you'd never have known it. The other lads didn't call him Sir. They called him Bill.

Bill pushed my chair along the paths.

"You'd be better off with electric, wouldn't you, sonny?" he said. "Some of the lads here use their Mobility Allowance to go electric. Then you could get around by yourself."

He showed me into the workshops where they teach skills and vocations. I saw boys wiring things up with brightly colored wires, hammering things of wood together. I saw boys stuffing cushions with kapok, and sorting colored pins into groups. I could do that if somebody showed me how.

Bill showed me the poolroom, the darts room, the gymnasium, the smoking area and the bar for the over-18's. He took me to the television room. But he won't ever catch me using that facility, not when there's so much other choice. I've watched more telly, side by side on the settee with my mum with a packet of chocolate digestives between us than most people in a lifetime.

Bill said, "D'you do signing? Makaton? Bliss? What signing do you use at home?"

"Yeerghaaarh," I said. I shook my head. It went round and round like the moon revolving on a stick. My mum says she can understand perfectly well what I need without needing to go waving her arms about in the air like some madman. My mum never learned signing. I never learned.

My mum was right in her way. In Makaton and Bliss where are those words for what I have to say? There is want and need and like and love and touch. Where is Man City and Manhood?

"Never mind," said Bill. "We'll manage." He bumped me up the ramp into the dormitory block.

"You'd have to learn to use the lift on your own," he said. "Press the button. Number three."

I have no numbers. I have colors.

"Top one. Blue."

I commanded my hand to rise and to press the button, but today the hand would not obey. This end-of-limb was not my slave. Bill did not help. He was speaking to someone outside the lift. They were behind me and I could not see them. I cannot turn my own head.

I growled to the hand. Reluctantly, the hand obeyed, or perhaps it was only chance.

"That's it," said Bill. "Good.

"Each student has his own cubicle," said Bill. "Nobody goes into any one else's without permission. O.K.? We try to show respect for others' privacy."

Bill knocked on a door which had a drawing of a black skull and crossbones pinned to it.

From inside a voice replied.

Bill opened the door a crack. "May we come in?" he asked. "Just showing round a new recruit."

"*May* we," he had asked. This respect was like a gift. No slave ever knocks on my door. At home, the door is always propped open with a chair.

"Just ajar, pet. Better that way. In case you need anything. You know I'm always there."

She has not had a full night's sleep since the day that I was born. I know because she had said as much on several occasions.

"But that's what mother-love is all about, lambkins."

29

He was a crumpled hunk, lounging across his bed, holding a picture postcard close to his eyes and smoking a thin black cheroot. The postcard was of a woman showing pieces of misplaced flesh and rounded body. I had never seen such a picture before but I knew what it was. There was also music in his room, wham, bam, wham that man, and the air was thick with the aromatic smoke.

Bill said, "Ashtray!" and chucked one onto the bed.

In that room, I saw things that I had been looking for all this time, but until this moment, I hadn't known what they were. There were posters on the wall and on the ceiling and on the door which showed people and guns and thighs and unexpected folds in the flesh. There were posters which showed toothpaste squirting from a tube, and suntan oil dribbling down warm shoulders. There were stallions running. And on the bedside locker, by his head, was a poster showing the cleft in the body where the legs meet inside the bushy curls.

These were the images I had been waiting to dream about. The boy on the bed had found them before me. I became excited on my chair and humped up and down. The strange sensation between my legs grew strong.

"Yeeeoorrgh!" I said.

"The rooms are mostly the same," said Bill. "You can do what you like. But you have to keep it tidy yourself. No one else does. Do they, Alid?"

The boy on the bed shrugged and flicked cheroot ash at the ashtray. He missed. It was his room. He could do as he pleased.

"You are coming here, you?" he said to me. Although his head swung as he spoke his eyes held contact with mine like magnets.

I waved my hands at him. I should've learned signing.

"Michael has got to do the assessment first," said Bill. "Like everybody else."

"See you around then," said the boy on the bed.

The assessment had been a worry. Yet it turned out to be perfectly feasible. I did O.K. The hands obeyed. The colored blocks balanced on other colored blocks. The nuts screwed onto the bolts. The left hand and the right hand knew each other. The eyes recognized images on the page.

"Which picture is the saucepan, Michael?"

At the image the head nodded.

"Well done. And which is the saucer?"

"Good. Now this one, Michael. Michael? Michael, can you hear? Flower, plant, pot or garden?"

Next, recognize printed words. I can't do printed words. But can he recognize his own written name? Yes, I know my own written name.

I am MAN CITY.

"So you can write your own name too? Why, that *is* good. Really good."

I became inflated by my success. I grabbed the crayon and wrote everything I knew. I wrote the zigs and the zags, the running lines and the straight. I wrote the gun shooting, the legs stretching, and the soft sheen on the sunburned bodyflesh.

And then it was time for lunch. Bill reappeared and wheeled me to the dining-block. In the dining-hall they had separate tables just like a restaurant. We could sit four to a table. Bill wheeled me to the serving-hatch and left me to sort out for myself. A serving lady carried my tray but there was nobody to feed me. I had to manage. Everyone else did.

I saw the cheroot boy from upstairs. He waved and his eyes saw mine. I waved. He came over to the table. He placed himself near me, so that when his elbow touched the frame of my wheelchair I could feel the warmth of him running through the cold metal tubing to reach my hand.

He had chosen rice and curried meat. I had chosen beans with chips. We smiled. I liked him. At St. John Chrysostom's we can choose our own meal.

He asked me, "You are coming here?"

I shook my head up and round and down.

"What you name then, you boy?"

"Mer. Mer," I said and then became angry that lips and throat and tongue would not obey and pronounce my name to my friend.

"Mermer?" he said. And then he saw my sweatshirt and he could read. "You mean Mermer Man City? That is a good name." And he laughed and touched the words on my shirt with his hand.

I laughed too and I nodded.

"I call you Man City then. That's O.K.?"

It was O.K.

After lunch, Bill returned for me and wheeled me to the toilets. He did nothing to assist. He left me to attend to it while he was occupied with his own pee. He seemed to ignore me. I wetted myself. I could not unfasten the velcro flies. I put myself into a wet mess. But I did not ask Bill for help. It was good to be alone like a man in the toilets. I do not like being pushed into the Ladies toilets by my mum. She says not to be a silly billy.

When we were back in the taxi with Mrs. Lovegrove and the driver, she kicked up a fuss.

"Oh really! They should've called me. Look at the state of you. I knew I shouldn't have let you go off on your own with that young man."

"Bill," I said and waved my hands. Does Bill keep pictures in his room?

It seemed such a long drive home. I was tired. So I was sick too. Mrs. Lovegrove suggested we stop at a hotel for a break.

"Unless you have something you need to be back for?"

"Well no," said my mum. "Not exactly. But I never like to be away from home too long. With a boy like my Michael, you never know, do you? Sometimes during the morning while he's at school I nip out. But never for long. I don't like to be out long. Just in case the bus is back early and that."

"Would you like a drink, Micky?" said Mrs. Lovegrove.

Yes, I'd like to drink the drink that men drink. When I go to St. John Chrysostom's they will teach me how to be a man and to drink like a man.

"He'll have a juice, if that's no trouble to you, Mrs. Lovegrove," said my mum. "He likes orange. It's good for his little system too."

My mum had the toweling bib round my neck in an instant. She had all the stuff I need in her carri-bag. When the drinks came, Mrs. Lovegrove lifted the glass of juice to my mouth.

"No, dear," said my mum. "He likes his own drinking straw better, don't you, pet?" She decanted the juice from the hotel's glass into my plastic beaker, inserted the special articulated plastic straw and held it for me to drink.

"You'd be surprised," said Mrs. Lovegrove, "how independent some of the lads become after only a term or two at St. John's."

"My Micky's never been away from me. I'm not sure he'd like it," said my mum. "There's all the little things he needs doing that only a mother knows."

"Of course, I dare say you'd miss him at first. But the staff find they come on such a lot, it's really worth it. Still, you don't have to make up your mind yet, do you? Not till you get the letter. There's three school-leaving dates each year, once he's reached sixteen."

So I waited for the letter to come, that letter from the

college which will release me from the slave-woman who dominates, who cares and protects, who represses, who believes that she owns me by virtue of having given me life.

"Up with your arms, pet. So we can pop your vest over your head. There's my good chappie!"

They'll be sending off that letter any day now, the letter to say when I shall start.

In the mornings, I lay as usual, as immobile as a rolled pork roast in my leg splints, my eyes closed to the baby bears, listening to the slave shuffling downstairs as she made her cup of tea and crushed my tablets with the back of a spoon.

But these days, as I waited for her to come up to my room and begin the ritual that starts each day, I no longer dreamed insubstantial dreams of chocolate biscuits. I dreamed of the touch of flesh, of the comfort of a body near to mine, of pleasure girls chosen in a market place and taken to the privacy of my own cubicle. My world was stretching beyond the cotton curtains. The sun-bronzed youth, now reaching the peak of his development, has many desires which all should be fulfilled.

I listened, each day, for the arrival of post flopping through the letter box and onto the mat. A big flop was mum's mail order catalogue, huge and heavy as a tombstone. She buys everything by direct order.

"We can't go getting out to the shops, see," she explained once to Mrs. Thingy. "Not like other people. Not with my little boy being the way he is. And all those stairs to go up. And all the people staring. Mind you, when I was younger, I was very fond of a spot of shopping."

When I am away at St. John's she will be able to go round the shops again, unencumbered. And while she shops, I will be learning skills. My slow mind will be taught to understand more quickly. My obstinate hands will be trained to obey, to whittle wood, to weave baskets. I will master the skill of dressing myself as other boys do, the skill of preparing my own medication. I will not mess around with childish concoctions of conserve. I will swallow down those tablets whole.

Downstairs, I ceased the ritual refusal of prunes and bran. Why resist what my body needs when the world of St. John's is there waiting?

"There's my good boy."

The slave can scarcely believe how co-operative I have become. She ruffled the long hair above my ears and I tolerated her treatment of me as an infant, knowing that it will not last much longer. When I am at St. John's I will have it short-cropped and manly, with a close-shaven neck, like the boy who smoked a cheroot and held a postcard of pieces of a woman.

Now I have so much. I have the future. I can afford to be compliant, gentle, tolerant with my carer.

Slavery is degrading to both slave and master. She too will surely be glad to be free of her bondage.

But waiting for the letter, time hangs suspended. I am waiting in the space between my life as a child, and my life as a man. And when the letter did not come I feared that perhaps they had forgotten me.

I knew she was anxious too. And then, at last it came. That morning, there were some brown envelopes, a brightly colored letter telling her about French windows, and a plain white typed envelope. That was the one. I knew it because she never receives white typed envelopes.

She was upstairs, fetching my muffler. I was in my chair, positioned beside the breakfast table. I know now how to make myself fall from my wheelchair. Head first from the chair is painful but I had to get to the letter, which I could see down the hallway and lying on the doormat. I propelled myself, wormlike, along the floor. My nodding head knocks against the wall. The carpet is rough as wirewool on the palms of my soft hands. I love the pain. I am Man City. I am worming wriggling free.

"Micky dear!" she called to me from upstairs. "What are you doing, pet?"

Instinctively, she knew that I was not where she had left me, not silent and still beside the empty cereal dishes. Does she know too how I have been practicing the carpet crawl?

"Micky pet!" she called from the top of the stairs. Then, "Oh no no!" for she saw me sprawling along the hall. She thought I had fallen. I left the other mail on the mat. I had the white typed envelope between my teeth. It was mine.

She rushed downstairs to me with her dressing gown flying like wings, and she gathered me up.

No, mum. No, leave me. Even squirming worms need freedom.

She doesn't leave me. She never leaves me. She enfolded me in the wings of her gown and I smell the strange smell of old worn-out woman.

"There's a kind boy. Trying to help your poor old ma. You needn't bother dear. I'll see to it after you've left for school."

She took it from me, and walked me back, one step, two step, to the sitting room. She did not open the envelope. Her hand was trembling as she held it, just like my hands tremble before *status epilepticus*. She carried the dishes across the kitchen to the sink. She flushed the tea-leaves from the teapot down the sink while the envelope lay out of reach on the table beside the branflakes.

Come along now, slave. Open it. Read it. Shout out the good news. Freedom. When do I start? The woodwork room. Body posters on the walls of my private cubicle. The cookery classes.

At long last she got around to reading it out loud for me to hear. At St. John Chrysostom's they teach many skills. Reading is a skill they may teach me. Hurry slave, before Bertram gets here.

" 'Dear Mrs. Graham,' " she reads. " 'We regret to inform you that a place is not available at this unit for your son Michael. After very careful consideration of his case, and of his particular needs, as well as close observation of him during his visit here, we feel that this unit is not able to offer him the high degree of supervision which he currently needs.' Well, thank goodness for that!"

I felt my face contort into a grimace. I wanted to cry, but instead I heard myself laughing like a hyena.

"Why Micky, pet, you're crying. What is it? Don't worry, pet. I wouldn't have let you go there. I won't ever let anyone take you away from me."

"Yeeerughaaah!" I cried out. Transplant me a new body so that they can see how I am Man City. Transplant me a voice so she can hear me cry for what I want. "Yeeraghuuh!" She puts her arms around me to re-enfold me in her suffocating embrace.

"It was a dustbin place, that dump. I'd never let them put you in a place like that. My own baby. I'll look after you always. That's mummy's promise."

Out in the street, the bus hooter sounded. Mrs. Thingy took up her post behind her lace curtain. The world revolved and the noise of the horn shrieked and resounded inside my head.

"There's Bertram now."

The jailer put on my jacket, and wheeled me to the door where Mrs. Lovegrove was ready to receive me. I am out on parole till four, and back in by nightfall. So it will be every day, every day for the rest of my life. My experience of the other kind of outer life out there was too fragile for me to be able to hold on.

"And what's up with our Micky Sunshine then?" said Bertram as Mrs. Lovegrove folded and loaded on board my chair. "Something really eating you up today, eh?"

"Don't take any notice of him," my mum called from the front step. "He just had a bit of a fright earlier on. Thought they'd come to take him away. Now he's just putting it on. Being an old silly billy. You know how he suffers from his bowels. He'll be right as rain once the prunes have done their work."

4

JONATHAN

On Sunday mornings Jonathan watched his family getting dressed up and he knew what it meant. It was time for church.

Jonathan liked going out with his family. But he didn't like having to have his hair brushed. And he hated having his face washed.

"Well, you can't go out with jam all around your mouth," said his mum.

"I don't expect God minds jam," said Jonathan's sister.

"No, but I do," said their mum. "Specially when it gets on the hymn books and makes them all sticky."

Jonathan's sister was ready to leave, and so was his dad. But Jonathan wasn't at all ready.

"Come along now, Jonathan!" said his mum. "Put on your shoes properly! You can't take forever or we'll all be late."

Jonathan was older than his sister but he couldn't do as many things as she could. And even the things he could do, like tying his own shoelaces, he did very slowly so that everybody had to stand and wait.

Sometimes, Jonathan liked going out. He liked being with

all the other people in church. He liked the singing. He liked the biscuits afterwards. Most of all, he liked it when the vicar was standing at the door and said, "Hello there, Jonathan, young fellow," and shook his hand.

But today they were late and the vicar wasn't there to welcome them. He had already gone inside to start the service. Jonathan felt annoyed. So he suddenly let go of his mum's hand and ran away.

"Oh no! No, no, no!" he called. "No church. Not today, thank you. I'm going to play hide-and-seek."

One of the things that Jonathan wasn't very good at was running away and hiding. It didn't take long for his mum to find him behind a yew tree in the graveyard.

Jonathan pretended he was invisible. But his mum was getting cross.

"It's really too much!" she said to Jonathan's dad. "Next Sunday he'll just have to stay behind with Mrs. Brett."

Mrs. Brett was their neighbor. Jonathan sometimes went to her house if his mum was very tired, or if his parents wanted to go out to see friends. Jonathan didn't like it much at Mrs. Brett's. She called him John, which wasn't his name, and he had to do jigsaws all the time and Mrs. Brett talked to him as though he were a baby.

"Oh no, mum!" said Jonathan's sister. "That's mean. He hates it there. Anyway, when we leave him behind at Mrs. Brett's, we aren't like a proper family any more."

She took hold of Jonathan's hand. "Please come on, Jonathan," she said. "They'll start singing the first hymn in a minute. You like the singing bit, don't you? D'you remember that alleluia hymn? You said it was like angels dancing."

Jonathan remembered.

"Come on then. It's much better if we all go in together."

Jonathan knew that his sister always wanted to help him, specially when other people didn't understand.

"Oh, all right," he said. So they all went in together.

But instead of a hymn with alleluias there was one which Jonathan didn't know and which went on for too long. So he felt inside his pocket for his money. He had a ten-pence piece which his mum had wrapped in a hanky so it wouldn't jingle. He took it out and rolled it along the shelf in front of him. It went like a car with only one wheel. Then it fell over the edge like a car having a crash. Jonathan crawled under the pew to look for it. He didn't find it but he found a glove and a piece of ribbon out of a hymn book instead.

"Look!" he said. He wanted to show them to his sister but the person in a big woolly hat just behind leaned forward, tapped him on the shoulder and said, "Shush!"

Jonathan's sister never shushed him, even when he woke her up very early by humming. She smiled at him now, while she was singing, and gave him her ten pence.

Jonathan put his sister's money into the glove and held it tight.

When he was little, Jonathan used to sit on his dad's knee while his sister sat on their mum's knee. Later, he used to go out with his sister and the other small children for a story in the vestry. But he was too old for that now. So he just had to sit. And sit. And sit.

His mum had her eyes shut. Perhaps she was busy praying. Perhaps she was just tired. His sister looked as though she was busy praying too. So was his father. Jonathan's own prayers never took very long. It was like the way he was with talking. He didn't have many things to say. Besides, he was always busy looking at things. He walked along to the end of the pew and looked at the metal radiator. It had feet, not two like a person, but four feet like a cat or a dog. When he tapped the top of the radiator with the ten-pence piece inside the old glove, it made a good noise like bells ringing.

Once, Jonathan's sister and his mum had been the people

who carried the bread and the wine and the money to the altar. Jonathan wasn't very good at carrying things, so he had sat with his dad and watched. He had been pleased to see his sister walking up the church with the tray of bread. He wished he could be important like that. He wished he could be useful. He knew he wasn't useful. Snotty Rebecca on the school bus had told him so.

"Useless, useless," she had said. "You're just useless, Jonathan dumb-brain."

"Lord in thy mercy," said the vicar.

"Hear our prayer," said all the people.

Jonathan looked at the tap which stuck out like a short metal tail on the radiator. Then he remembered that he knew the bit about hearing our prayer.

"Hear our prayer," he said slowly. But he was too late. Everyone else was on to another part. The lady in the pew behind glared at him as he sidled back to his seat.

Jonathan liked it when it was time to queue up at the front of the church. Being close together with all the people was good, like waiting in line for dinner at school. Jonathan saw the shiny candlesticks on the altar and the candles burning. He watched the boys in the choir. They were singing usefully. He felt the vicar's hand on his head blessing him. Then he walked back to his place clutching his dad's arm.

"Careful now," he said to his dad as they went down the steps.

The steps were slippy. Once, a long time ago, Jonathan had tripped coming down them and yelled with fright.

After the service, there was coffee and biscuits in the vestry so that all the grown-ups could talk to each other. Jonathan let go of his dad's arm, went to the table and took a biscuit from the edge of the plate. One of the ladies who made the coffee patted his sister's head.

"What a dear little poppet. Always so good and quiet."

People never said what a dear little poppet Jonathan was. Instead, they said, "Really, I don't know why they bring that boy in week after week." Jonathan knew they were talking about him again.

Jonathan's sister heard it too and it made her sad. She knew that when Jonathan drummed his shoes on the floor, and jingled his money, it was like him trying to sing or hum. He didn't do it to annoy people on purpose. She fetched Jonathan three more biscuits.

"Come on, Jonathan," she said, "Let's go outside and look at the graves."

Jonathan always liked that.

He sat in the long grass and listened while his sister read the names off the stone tombs.

"Thomas Bellamy. Benjamin Freeman. Josiah Franklin. Louisa Perry."

"Funny names," said Jonathan.

"Yes. They're very old, too," said his sister. "The people died years and years ago, long before we were even born."

Jonathan could see the stones were old because they were covered in moss. His favorite stone was half fallen over with green creepers growing over it. His sister read it for him.

"Jonathan Buckworthy. Departed this life 1882."

"That one's my name."

"Yes, Jonathan is," said his sister. "But not Buckworthy. I wonder who he was."

Sometimes Jonathan wished he could read names on stones all by himself.

"Reading doesn't matter that much," said his sister. "When we get to heaven, we'll all be the same. We won't need to read. Just like when we're babies, we're all about the same."

The grown-ups had finished their coffee and were coming out of the vestry.

"Who's that?" Jonathan asked his sister as each person came out.

He watched a lady with a nice round face come out and stand talking to the vicar.

"And that?"

"I don't know. Never seen her before. Maybe she's just moved here."

But Jonathan was sure he had seen her before, only he couldn't think where.

"Why d'you think I should know who everybody is?" said his sister.

The lady went on smiling towards him and then she came right over.

"Hello there, Jonathan," she said. "Remember me? I used to serve dinners at school. I used to see you every day, didn't I? I remember you always liked seconds of sprouts."

And Jonathan thought he probably remembered. She used to wear a checkered overall and a cotton check cap. Now she wasn't. That's why he didn't recognize her.

"D'you still like lots of sprouts?"

Jonathan couldn't remember.

"I work in a different school now. My baby grandson's being christened at this church next weekend."

Jonathan wondered where the baby was. He hadn't noticed any babies.

"No, he's not here today. He makes such a noise. Besides, it seemed a bit cold to bring him out today. He's only little."

Jonathan was glad he wasn't little and having to stay in because of the cold.

"I'm not cold," he said.

The dinner lady said, "My son-in-law sings in the choir. I expect you know him. He knows you."

Jonathan couldn't remember but he nodded all the same. "He wondered if you'd like to come and help us get the church ready on Friday?"

Jonathan didn't know what to say.

"Go on, Jonathan, say yes," said his sister. So Jonathan said yes. And the dinner lady said,

"Great. I'll check with your mum that it's all right. D'you want to come along too?" she asked Jonathan's sister.

"No thanks. I've got Brownies on Fridays."

So on Friday afternoon as soon as Bertram's bus had brought Jonathan home from school, Jonathan's dad took him round to the church. Jonathan's new friend, the dinner lady, had come straight from work, so she was still wearing her green check overall. Jonathan recognized her at once. She, and her son-in-law, and her daughter and the vicar were talking about the christening. But when she saw Jonathan, she came over to him. The baby was there too asleep in a pram. Jonathan thought how dull it must be, being a baby and not being able to see anything or do anything.

"I'm glad you've come, Jonathan," she said. "We need someone useful. There's several things to be done. Would you be able to put out the hymn books?"

She showed Jonathan what to do. He had to fetch the books from a big chest and put one book and one piece of white paper with musical notes on it in each place, so that everybody would know when to sing and when to listen during the baby's christening. It was a difficult job for a boy like Jonathan who was a dumb-brain and wasn't any good at counting or numbers or carrying things.

Jonathan really wanted to do this useful job right. At first, he tried to do it as fast as he could. But he dropped a pile of hymn books on the floor. It made quite a noise but luckily nobody took any notice. He started again very slowly and carefully, taking one book at a time and making sure that each one was facing the right way and was quite straight. Even though he could not read words, he knew when letters were upside down or the right way up.

When he had put books and music sheets in all the front rows, the dinner lady and her family were still busy talking to the vicar, so Jonathan fetched some more books from the chest and, by the time the dinner lady was ready to talk to Jonathan again, he had put a hymn book in every place in the whole church, even in the dusty old pews at the back where nobody ever sat.

"Well done, Jonathan. That *does* look good," said the dinner lady. Jonathan thought it looked good too, to see so many books all around the church and to know he had put every one out himself.

"Bet a little baby couldn't do that," he thought.

Next, he helped to fetch jugs of clean water for the flowers from a tap outside.

"Now, last job of all," said the dinner lady. "They're choosing which hymns to sing."

Jonathan wondered if the baby in the pram outside would be allowed to choose a hymn all by itself.

The dinner lady said, "What's your favorite, Jonathan?"

Jonathan thought about it. It was hard when people asked him questions. He could never think of a right answer. Then he remembered a hymn which he had thought sounded like angels dancing.

"All creatures, alleluia," he said, "That's my best."

"I don't think I know that one," said the dinner lady.

Jonathan wasn't very good at talking but now that he'd decided what his favorite hymn was, he got better at remembering it. He said, "O praise him, O praise him, O praise him, alleluia, alleluia, alleluia."

"Oh, *I* know the one you mean!" said the dinner lady. "You must mean *All Creatures of Our God and King*. Is that the one?"

When the dinner lady's son-in-law hummed the tune, Jonathan thought he remembered it even better.

"Good," said the vicar. "That's always a great favorite. We'll all enjoy that, I'm sure."

Just then Jonathan's dad arrived to take Jonathan home again.

"Jonathan's been so useful," said the dinner lady to Jonathan's dad. "You will be coming along tomorrow, to the christening, won't you? And we'll have some tea afterwards, back at my place."

Jonathan's dad said they would.

Jonathan couldn't remember ever going to a christening before.

"Course you've been to one," said his sister. "You must have been to mine, when I was a baby. And your own. That's when you got given your name."

Jonathan didn't think he could remember his own christening.

"Course you can't. You're not meant to," said his sister. "You were only a baby. Most people can't remember back to when they were babies."

The next day, Jonathan took off his shoes, put on his best (red stripey) socks, and put his shoes back on. He brushed his own hair. When he and his family reached the church, they were shown to a good place right beside the font so that Jonathan and his sister could see properly. The hymn books were just how Jonathan had put them the day before. The flowers were in the vases round the font. There were already quite a few people sitting waiting in the church. The baby was there too, still sleeping in its pram.

"Hello, Jonathan," said the dinner lady. Her son-in-law and her daughter came and said hello to him too.

The baby had white flowers tied to the pram handle, and it was wearing a white lace dress and bonnet. When they took it out of its pram and Jonathan could see its face better, he thought it looked like the most ugly thing he had ever seen.

He felt glad that he didn't look like that.

As soon as the service started, the baby began to yell. It yelled and yelled. Even when the vicar was saying the prayers and everyone was meant to be quiet, it went on crying. For someone so small, it made a very loud noise, the biggest noise Jonathan had ever heard in a church. Its face went bright red. Several people said "Shush" to the baby but it didn't take any notice. Jonathan thought it was so wonderful that he drummed his shoes on the floor. Jonathan was glad it didn't stop yelling even when they told it to shush.

It was a boy baby and was to be named Mark John William.

"That's three names," Jonathan said to his sister. "Three's a lot of names."

"I expect it's in case it doesn't like the first one," said his sister. "Then it can change to one of the others."

Jonathan thought he wouldn't want to have to change his name. He liked his name.

"I'm Jonathan, aren't I?" he said to his sister.

"Yes."

"I won't have to change?"

"No."

When the baby had been christened, the people sang the hymn which Jonathan had chosen, *All Creatures of Our God and King*, using the hymn books which Jonathan had put out. Jonathan shouted "Alleluia! Alleluia! Alleluia!" as loudly and cheerfully as he could because he knew that the baby, Mark John William, liked lots of happy noises, and so does God.

The hymn was so loud and so cheerful that the baby

suddenly stopped yelling and lay quite still, smiling up at the candles. Everybody was very surprised.

The Sunday after the christening, Jonathan got himself dressed and ready long before his dad or his mum or his sister. He had to tell them to hurry up or they'd be late.

He wanted to get there in good time. He wanted to see his friend the dinner lady again. But when they arrived, he was sad to find she wasn't there.

Jonathan's sister said, "But look, there's plenty of other people here. I'm sure you can still help with the books."

So Jonathan stood beside the vicar at the door and handed out hymn books for everybody who arrived, and some of the people smiled and said, "Thank you, Jonathan."

And during the dull bits of the service, Jonathan was very happy thinking about how busy he'd be collecting up the books afterwards.

When the vicar said, "Lord in thy mercy," Jonathan said "Hear our prayer," as loudly as he could without actually shouting.

"I think Jonathan's really pleased," said his sister afterwards. "Now that he's got such a useful job to do. Aren't you?"

Jonathan thought he was.

"You could have a new name now if you wanted to," said his sister. "Jonathan, The Book Helper."

5

MARILYN AND FLEUR

▪ MARILYN'S STORY ▪

No one likes Marilyn. Gangling Marilyn's a fidget and a drip.

People don't like Marilyn because of her drips. She drips from her nose, and from her panties. She dribbles drips from the corners of her mouth, down onto her patterned pastel sweater. Chiefly she drips from her eyes. Marilyn is a teenaged cry-baby. Marilyn is always feeling sorry for herself.

This story is meant to be Fleur's. But Marilyn will have to be in it too because otherwise she'll feel left out. Fleur and Marilyn always sit together on the bus, side by side, at the back, Fleur nearest the window, Marilyn nearest the aisle. No one, apart from Fleur, ever wants to sit next to Marilyn. Fleur, dainty as a woodland flower, is already on board the school bus, her hands neatly crossed, her sandwich box on her lap.

Marilyn is waiting for the bus, standing with her mother on the corner of Queen's Drive South. She clutches an important crocodile-skin handbag to her front. Marilyn is microcephalic, with a head so small that kids on their way to the Elizabeth the Second comprehensive, call out "Hi there, Pinhead!" as they cycle past. Marilyn's feet are uneven, one sized 4½, the other sized 6, these mismatched feet attached to weak and wobbly ankles. Her eyes are not in alignment. She sees the world differently from the way that flowerlike Fleur sees it. With her crooked eyes, she sees it sour and yellow.

As she is guided up the steps onto the bus by Mrs. Lovegrove, the bus escort, Marilyn begins to whimper, then to weep. Because it is not fair. She has heard her mother say so, time and again.

"Is it fair, I ask you, is it, that my poor wee girlie, in addition to all her other misfortunes, has to travel with those awful paraplegics? They're just louts, a threat to any decent society. It's not safe, I know it isn't, my poor Marilyn on the bus with them. They should be castrated, that's what I say. It's the only way to stop them. They ought to put them on separate buses. Not go expecting children like our Marilyn to travel on the same transport."

Every day, Marilyn is learning from her parents how the world has been unjustly cruel to them, while shining with kindness on many less deserving families.

"Like that Micky for a start. I know for a fact *his* mother gets the Mobility Allowance. That's twenty odd pounds a week. And what happened to us when we applied? What did they say? They said Marilyn's got her feet, that's what they said. Mobility's only for people with no feet. But what sort of feet do they think Marilyn's are, I ask you? That Micky's mother gets Mobility Allowance and a bus to take her son to school. What's she want all that cash for, that's what I'd like to know. She ought to be made to use it towards separate transport."

Marilyn's father, lighting his pipe, says, "I don't think anyone knows really what it's been like for my wife. Nobody really understands how much we've suffered from discriminations."

Marilyn climbs on board and stumbles along the aisle towards the back of the bus, from where Fleur smiles and nods so that Marilyn will know she's saved her a place. Marilyn doesn't return the smile. Marilyn knows that, as a deprived and pin-headed person, she must give away nothing, least of all a smile.

"Misery me, misery me," feels she to herself, angrily sitting down and twisting the worn straps of her handbag. "Andy, Jonathan, Micky. Hate, misery, hate. Poor little Marilyn. Not fair not fair."

It is Micky she hates most of all. The worst of the deviant bunch, as her mother has repeatedly told her. Two stops further on, Micky is waiting on the narrow pavement outside his home at Empire Villas. First his wheelchair in at the back of the bus, then he is heaved bodily up the steps, a task which doesn't do Mrs. Lovegrove's back any good at all. In four years' time she is going to be forced to take early retirement because of the damage done to her spine from lifting heavy lads.

However, any concern for a bus escort's arthritic vertebrae is far from Marilyn's thoughts. Instead, misery and hate is mounting to panic as Micky, now seated in his place, begins his morning pantomime. First the loud uncouth noises. Then the rolling of his eyes in the coarse manner that would give Marilyn's mother heartburn if she were unlucky enough to witness it. Finally, Micky lunges across with his flippy-floppy hands to tweak at Marilyn's handbag and he laughs loudly in her face. Micky knows that what Marilyn keeps in her copious bag, the used Kleenex tissue, the worn felt-tip pen, the empty Smarties tube, is holding Marilyn together.

"Micky, dear," says Mrs. Lovegrove, turning round in her seat to supervise those behind as well as in front. "Leave Marilyn's bag alone, there's a good lad. And give her back her Smarties box. You know she likes to keep it safe." But even Mrs. Lovegrove finds Marilyn a difficult child to love as she sniffs and drips and fidgets on her lap with the dried-up skin of a long-dead-reptile handbag on the seat beside gentle Fleur.

Be thankful for small mercies, Mrs. Lovegrove reminds herself. For never was there such a runner-awayer as Marilyn used to be, when she was younger. Forever darting here, there and everywhere. At least these days she stays still in one place. How that little Fleur puts up with it, goodness only knows. Never says a thing. Always so good.

As soon as the bus starts moving, Marilyn releases the intensity of her feelings on the nearest object, namely Fleur, with a finger-pinch on Fleur's cheek as rapid as a blink, so nobody sees it happen. After all, unlike the common housefly, Mrs. Lovegrove can't have eyes on all sides of her head. Fleur flinches, but doesn't retaliate, doesn't cry out. Worse things than this have happened to her, way back in the past. And better things too.

Fleur tolerates Marilyn's taunts, not because she is weak, but because, these days, she is strong. And what happened in Fleur's life to change her from a small, scratched, frightened person into a small strong person is her favorite story, which she likes to think over to herself from time to time, especially when she's seated beside big Rob before a dancing wood fire. So let us hear it now.

▪ FLEUR'S STORY ▪

If Fleur spoke, this is the story she might tell.

Once upon a time, there was a somebody called Fleur. Fleur did not like to talk. Fleur did not like to walk. Fleur did not like to run. Fleur did not like to think. Fleur always sat quietly in the same place with her back to the wall, her eyes to the window. Fleur needed the light. Long ago, before Fleur was brought to this place, Fleur was in another place where it was dark. Fleur needed the curtains too, into whose soft safety Fleur could retreat when the world became noisy.

Fleur was not safe with people. Fleur had no parents that Fleur wanted to remember. When Fleur tried to remember things, or think things, Fleur's thoughts were muddled and distressing. Fleur could not always remember who she was, or why Fleur was. Fleur did not want to remember. Fleur wanted to sit by a window.

These days, Fleur lived in a large household filled with many children who came and went, went and came. They were changing. Sometimes they rode bicycles around the gardens, fed the guinea-pig, teased the rabbit, drew pictures, and read stories. Few of the other children remained at the big house for long. Adult people came and talked to them and took them away. Fleur watched them going off and never saw them coming back. Fleur always stayed.

At night, Fleur slept in a dormitory with six beds and sometimes five other children and sometimes no other children, and Fleur always had the bed near the window so Fleur could reach the light. Fleur needed to be near the light with Fleur's back to the wall and with the curtains near. By day, Fleur sat by the big window of the playroom looking out at the garden. That was where Fleur was safe, where Fleur could see the sun and the big sky and the flowering plum trees. Fleur watched the birds in the trees.

"That child ought to have some people of her own," Fleur heard the woman say to one of the other women. She was the woman who looked after the other women who looked after the children, whom Fleur had heard called Miss Ream Duty Staff. But Fleur did not call her anything because Fleur did not like to speak. But Fleur could hear and Fleur could see. As Fleur sat by the window of the playroom, Fleur could see birds in the tree and could hear them too. Fleur was watching the birds. "You'd like that, wouldn't you Fleur?" said the Missreamdutystaff.

Fleur thought about the birds as they ran from branch to branch like fleas hopping, but happier than fleas, like children playing but freer than children. Fleur said nothing. Were the birds afraid? There were many birds chattering in the tree, just as there were many children at the big place where chattering children lived.

"To go and live with a family of your very own, like Darren did? You remember Darren?"

Fleur remembered Darren. He went away with the people who have given him his own blue bicycle. Fleur did not want a bike. Fleur wanted to sit by the window.

"Of course you would, dear. A nice new mummy and daddy all of your own. Everybody needs some nice parents of their own. I shall go off to my office and see what can be done about it. I'm sure there's a lovely mummy just waiting for you somewhere."

And, sure enough, what the Missreamdutystaff said should happen, did happen.

One day, after school, a woman and a man visited. Fleur saw them get out of their car, and saw their lips moving as they spoke to the Missreamdutystaff. Fleur knew that they had not come to inspect any of the other children because they were not looking at the other children riding bicycles, feeding the guinea-pig or drawing at the table. Fleur knew they had come to visit Fleur because Fleur could see them glancing up at Fleur as Fleur sat by the window. Fleur looked out at the fleas hopping on the tree and tried not to think of the small dark cupboard under the stairs. There were fleas in the cupboard. And rags. And smells. And fear. And once there was the sound of a bird struggling inside the wall where it had come down the chimney and was trapped in the dark just like Fleur and it rattled its wings till it died. Fleur never died.

No one at this place where Fleur lived now ever spoke of that cupboard, of the darkness inside the cupboard where Fleur used once to live, of the shouting outside, and the flapping of sooty wings inside. Fleur did not know if they knew. Did anyone know about the shouting of the mummy and daddy just outside the cupboard?

"God you're so stupid! Can't you do anything right?"

Fleur's mummy and Fleur's daddy were angry people who hauled Fleur by the arm to the cupboard beside the fireplace and made Fleur crawl inside and then the door was closed behind Fleur and Fleur was alone in the dark.

"That child's so stupid! Why's that child so stupid? If you don't shout at her she just sits there, staring into space."

"Like some moron."

"In God's name, why can't she *do* something, like other people's children?"

"She's not even clean. At *her* age! It's disgusting!"

"I can't bear it, you know. I can't take it much longer."

"So *you* can't take it? What about me? I'm with her all day long."

"You know where it comes from, don't you? And it's not my side of the family. I can tell you that. It's that aunt of yours. It has to be. The one that was put away."

Fleur saw the Missreamdutystaff lead the woman and the man up the steps of the big house and inside. Fleur heard them in the hall.

The Missreamdutystaff was not like a mummy or daddy for she did not change her mind, she did not hit children, she did not scream in your ears, she did not drag children away and bundle them into a small dark cupboard. The Missreamdutystaff was more like a safe high wall. She was large and secure.

The visitors were talking in the hall, about one of the children who was to be visited and taken away.

"From the photos we've seen, she seems a pretty little poppet," Fleur heard the woman say.

"And bright as a button, I'd say," said the man. "From the pictures, that is."

The Missreamdutystaff sent photographs of children to people who might want to have them. They were displayed on the Missreamdutystaff's office wall. Fleur had once been taken to a shop where there were sweets and chocolate and biscuits you could choose. Fleur had chosen a tube of sweet-tasting rainbow discs in a colored cardboard tube. The pictures pinned to the Missreamdutystaff's office wall were like sweets on the shelves in the shop. The couples could come and choose. Some people like some kind of taste and wrapping. Others preferred another. Among the pictures on the Missreamdutystaff's wall was one of a girl with blond wispy hair and faraway eyes. Underneath it said FLEUR. Fleur didn't look at that one. Fleur was Fleur, here inside Fleur's self. Fleur would not be the beautiful child without a smile pinned up on the wall.

"Yes, she's very attractive," said the Missreamdutystaff. "But you mustn't let her looks mislead you."

"The poor wee mite. How could any parents do such things to a little child?"

"She can't really be all that retarded," said the man. "In the picture there's such a keen look in her eye."

"So what are the drawbacks? Behavior and so on?"

"None at all, really," said the Missreamdutystaff. "Although she is, as I explained, intellectually retarded, she has few serious behavioral problems apart from withdrawal. In fact, considering the unsettled past, what happened before, she's surprisingly well-adjusted. Sometimes these less able children are, in a way, protected by their limitations from understanding too much. Which is probably just as well. Of course, she doesn't speak yet, maybe she never will. And she's small for her age. This may well be due to malnutrition. But you know it's amazing how children like this often seem to put on a growth spurt the moment they're settled into new homes. You can almost see the change in them."

Fleur watched the Missreamdutystaff bring the couple across the playroom. They did not go to any other child. They came to Fleur. The Missreamdutystaff said to Fleur,

"Fleur, dear, this gentleman and this lady would like to be your new mummy and daddy."

"Oh my! The little scrappet!" said the lady, clapping her hands together. "Isn't she a sweetie!"

Fleur was as small as a fairy, with fine fairy-like hair, and thin pixie-like legs.

Fleur looked at Fleur's legs.

The birds have thin legs like these, thought Fleur. And the thought didn't frighten Fleur until she remembered that birds can be trapped in dark places, will make a noise until they die. Fleur would make no noise.

Fleur looked at the man and the woman. The woman did not look like the other woman who used to push her into the darkness where the bird had flapped, where the fleas had hopped.

"You've always wanted a kind mummy and daddy, haven't you, dear?" said the Missreamdutystaff.

And Fleur wondered if Fleur had. It was hard to know.

The lady reached out her hand and patted Fleur on the top of her wispy head. The gentleman chuckled and smiled.

They didn't sound like those other people who used to lock her in the darkness in the cupboard under the stairs.

"We've got a lovely home," said the lady, glancing up at the Missreamdutystaff. "With a Wendy house and a climbing frame. We'll get you a bike as soon as you're ready."

"That's right," said the gentleman. "We've got lots of toys back at our place."

The Missreamdutystaff said, "Fleur doesn't need a lot of toys. She doesn't really get a lot out of playing. It's love she needs most of all. You'll probably find at first she prefers just sitting and watching the world."

"Oh, but we want to give her all the good things of life!" said the lady. "After all she's been through, we want to make it up to her. My neighbor's dressing her a lovely Sindy doll, with all the outfits. Isn't she, dear?" She looked at her husband.

The lady took Fleur's hand and Fleur went with them in their car back to their house. They took Fleur upstairs, the lady just in front, the man just behind, and showed Fleur the bedroom where Fleur would sleep. It was not dark in the bedroom. Fleur was glad. There was a window. Fleur went to the window but found that it had net curtains like white clouds hung over it so that Fleur couldn't see through to the outside.

"Don't pull at the drapes like that, dear," said the lady. "Or the whole pelmet may come down. And that wouldn't be very nice, would it?"

Fleur didn't know.

There was also a cupboard in the bedroom, set into the wall beside the fireplace. Fleur didn't like to look at the cupboard. There were pictures on the walls of rats in funny top hats.

"We got them specially framed for you. D'you like them? They're rather fun, aren't they? Mr. and Mrs. Rat and all their children."

They went downstairs, the gentleman just in front, the lady just behind, and they gave Fleur the toys.

"Look, Fleur," said the lady. "Look what we got for you in the shop!"

The lady took the toy from its box and wound it up and made it jerk across the carpet. But Fleur wanted to be near a window to see out and watch the sky.

"You can call me mummy, if you like," said the lady. "And you may call Mr. Hickson daddy."

The window downstairs had thick white curtains too. Fleur couldn't see out.

"Careful, dear," said the lady.

"Maybe the clockwork frog frightened her?" said the daddy gentleman. The mummy said,

"Look Fleur, see here, dear. Here's the nice friendly poodle. He won't hurt you. See daddy wind doggy up and make him sit up and beg for his bone. Watch daddy."

The lady and the gentleman crouched down on the carpet and played with their clockwork poodle.

Fleur thought, Fleur needs the window. But the thick white clouds at the window stifled it and shut out the sky.

"D'you want to stay here for always and be our own little girl?" asked the lady, as she brushed Fleur's fair hair next morning and tied it with pink ribbons in two tight bunches, one on each side of her head.

Fleur thought, Yes. Fleur was a little girl and Fleur was here and Fleur liked the window upstairs in the bedroom, if only Fleur could see out through the net clouds to the sky. Fleur smiled and Fleur smiled. These people didn't shout at Fleur or lock Fleur in dark places. They fed Fleur and they bathed Fleur and they sat Fleur on their laps and showed Fleur things, and showed Fleur things and showed Fleur things.

"Good girl. Now then, if you want to be our little girl, you must try just a teeny weeny bit harder. Just a little bit harder than you have done so far. All right?"

Fleur, sitting on the carpet with the lady and gentleman's toys, felt for a tiny thread of wool in the carpet. Fleur pulled it and pulled it and eased it out of the carpet and rolled it between her fingers. The lady didn't see.

"Here's the jigsaw puzzle we tried yesterday. Remember the nice picture of the big chuffer train? I'll help you with it now and tomorrow you'll see if you can fit it together all by yourself. I know you can if you try. You've got such a lot of catching up to do."

"Jij-see," said Fleur because it seemed to please the lady and make her happy to hear Fleur say it. "Jij-see, Fleur jij-see, jij-see, jij-see, jij-see."

"Yes, that's right, but you don't have to keep saying it, you know."

"Jij-see," said Fleur and Fleur thought of the window upstairs. If Fleur could only see through it there would be sky and trees and birds running along the branches.

They never shouted at Fleur like the other people long ago outside the cupboard, not once. As they guided Fleur out to the car and helped Fleur into the back seat, they were quite silent. The gentleman drove. The lady sat beside him, not speaking. All the toys were piled up beside Fleur on the seat, the clockwork poodle, the wind-up frog, the jigsaws and the spinning top, tidily in their boxes.

"We'll have to let her keep the toys," the lady had said. "We got them for her, specially, didn't we?"

The gentleman agreed that the toys and Fleur should stay together.

"We couldn't very well offer them to another child, not now they've been used, could we?"

Fleur pulled a piece of thread from the seat cover and rolled it between her fingers. Fleur did not let Fleur's eyes look up to see out of the window at the passing houses, the passing buses, the passing traffic lights. Fleur rolled the thread carefully and put it in Fleur's mouth and Fleur looked down at Fleur's tiny neat feet side by side on the car floor, which was carpeted and very very clean. Fleur did not know where Fleur was traveling to in the clean car with the toys and Fleur was frightened that this gentleman and the lady would put Fleur in the dark. They didn't speak and Fleur knew that Fleur had displeased them in some way.

"We can't keep her," said the lady to the Missreamdutystaff when they reached the place with the many other children who came and went where Fleur used to live. "It's not that we don't like her. It's not that at all. We've tried to make it work. Lord, have we tried!"

The gentleman nodded.

"What's wrong, then?" the Missreamdutystaff asked. "What did she do? Funny, I've never known her to misbehave before. Withdrawn but manageable."

"She didn't *do* anything," said the lady. "That's the trouble."

"She's a no-hoper," said the gentleman. "She just sits all day, looking pretty and staring."

"We've offered her so much," said the lady. "She just won't respond."

"If only she'd lied. Or stolen. Or thrown a tantrum, then we could've coped. We're very experienced parents, you know."

"*And* she eats curtains! All my new net curtains, picked to tatters. You never told us she had weird habits."

"I'm afraid she's just not the daughter for us. We're very sorry."

Fleur, clutching the Missreamdutystaff's skirt. Fleur easing out a loose thread from inside the pocket of Fleur's dress. Fleur rolling it into a ball, pushing it into Fleur's left ear. Now Fleur couldn't hear them speaking. Fleur crossed to the window. Fleur leaned against the wall. Fleur rocked herself roughly from side to side, deaf and blind, safe in the darkness of a cupboard she made around herself.

Now the Missreamdutystaff was always talking about Fleur to the other staff, watching Fleur, worrying about Fleur. Fleur knew. And Fleur knew that because Fleur had once, long ago, lived in a dark cupboard, nobody wanted Fleur. Other children came and went. Fleur remained.

"Thick," thought Fleur to herself. One of the children shouted this to Fleur as Fleur sat by the window pulling threads from the hem of the curtain. Fleur heard him.

"Thick!" said Fleur out loud. The Missreamdutystaff was surprised. Fleur rarely spoke.

"Thick," Fleur said again.

"You're not thick, dear. You're Fleur," said the Missreamdutystaff and to one of the staff she said, "We must try harder to get that child adopted. She's beginning to lose confidence in herself."

There was a blind boy at the children's home. Fleur knew he was blind. For him, his hands were his windows. With his hands he felt an orange. With his hands he touched. With his hands, Darren saw.

Were all the boys who came here called Darren? Fleur wondered.

"Not Darren, dear. The new little boy's called Darryl."

Sometimes Darryl came and sat by Fleur at the window. But he couldn't see Fleur's sky, Fleur's sun. Because he couldn't see anything, Fleur let him stay. And sometimes she eased out a thread from the hem of the long curtain and gave it to him to look at with his hands.

A woman and a man came. Fleur thought they had come for her. They were talking to the Missreamdutystaff and looking across the room at Fleur.

Fleur grabbed hold of Darryl's seeing hand and pulled him across the room and pushed him at the man and the woman.

"Darryl!" Fleur said. "Take Darryl. Take blind Darryl. Darryl jij-sees. Not Fleur! Not Fleur!"

"Fleur, dear," said matron. "This lady and gentleman don't want Darryl. It's you they've come to see."

Fleur did not want to go with them.

"It's all right, dear," said the Missreamdutystaff. "You're not going anywhere. They'd just like to stay for tea and get to know you."

The lady and gentleman stayed for tea and grinned and grinned at Fleur.

"Goodbye, Fleur," they said when they left. "See you again next weekend."

Fleur didn't know what a weekend was. The man and the lady didn't ever come back and see Fleur, so Fleur never found out about a weekend.

A blind man with a dog in a harness came to see Darryl. Like all the other children, Darryl went away too and never came back to sit with Fleur at the window. Fleur was alone.

"Sometimes," said the Missreamdutystaff, "I wish that little girl would scream, and bite, and attack people, and throw plates of spaghetti across the room. Parents seem to feel they can cope better with that sort of thing. It's more of a challenge to them, I suppose."

• ROB'S STORY •

Now here comes another good story, one that Fleur didn't know about before. But she knows about it now because Rob tells it sometimes as they sit quietly by the fire. So Fleur has it for always inside her head to remember whenever she wants. The first time that Fleur heard Rob's story, she smiled and shuffled with contentment on her seat by the fire.

Rob and Ruby lived near a farm. Rob worked on the farm for the farmer. Rob and Ruby had Angela, David, Lizzie, Nevil, Jane, and Andrew. These children did not come and go and change their names or faces like the children at Fairlawns Children's Home where Fleur was living, but stayed all the time with Rob and Ruby and never went away, except to school in the morning, but they always came back in time for tea. Rob and Ruby lived in a cottage with three bedrooms. Rob and Ruby slept in one bedroom. Nevil, David, and Andrew slept in another. Lizzie, Jane, and Angela slept in the other. And there was still room in the girls' room for another person to sleep in the little bed under the window.

"We should find another person," said Angela to Lizzie.

"We could ask Rob and Ruby about it," said Angela.

Ruby and Rob knew where to find children because they had already found Angela, David, Lizzie, Nevil, Jane, and Andrew.

"Yes, we've got a little girl," said the voice of the duty staff on the telephone to Rob when he rang from the telephone kiosk. "But she's not a very rewarding child."

And Fleur, hearing about it afterward in Rob's story, smiled because whatever that had once meant was over and done with now.

"She doesn't give a lot back," said the voice of the duty staff.

"Ah, well," said Rob.

"And she's a picker."

"A picker?" said Rob.

"She picks holes in things all the time."

"Ah, well," said Rob. "We've got hens out in the yard. They're a bit like that when they're unhappy."

"And she doesn't speak a lot," the voice said. "In fact she doesn't speak at all these days."

"We're not much of speakers ourselves," said Rob. "We live a quiet life. We couldn't offer her very much. What with the six of them already, we're not well off. Though we make do."

"And she's very shy of strangers."

"Funny that. So's my Ruby. That's why she likes it where we are now, out at the farm. We're way off the main road here. And off the main drainage, though we've got the electrics in now."

"I'm not sure if you understand me. Fleur's had two failed placements. She doesn't trust anybody. And we don't even know how much she understands."

"Ah, well," said Rob. "We'll come and take a peek anyway, if that's all right?"

So, on a windy spring day, Rob borrowed a truck from the farmer on whose land they lived, and drove with Ruby to Fairlawns Children's Home. They arrived an hour early. So they sat in their truck parked outside the gates, looking out through the truck windows at the fast-moving sky and the blowing trees, and drinking tea from a thermos flask which Ruby had brought until it was time to go in and meet Miss Ream.

"You go in first," said Ruby. "I'll wait out here."

So Rob went in and Miss Ream took him to the children's playroom where a small child was standing by the window.

"She spends a lot of time just staring out of the window," said Miss Ream.

But Rob could see how the child wasn't really looking out at anything for she had her head tucked inside her jersey and she was chewing pieces of thread pulled from the curtains.

"This is Rob," said Miss Ream.

"Hello," said Rob.

The child looked at him through the holes of her jersey. But she didn't say anything. So Rob went back out to the truck. Ruby went in next. Fleur was still standing by the window with her head pulled inside her jersey like a tortoise inside its shell, a bird inside a sooty chimney, a Fleur inside a cupboard.

"This is Ruby," said Miss Ream.

Ruby saw Fleur looking out through the holes in the knitting. Neither of them said anything. But Fleur came out of her jersey for a moment. Ruby still didn't say anything, so they both looked out of the window for a while at the clouds dashing by and then Ruby went with Miss Ream to her office and Rob joined them there.

"I'm afraid she doesn't really seem to think much of either of us," Rob said sadly. "We couldn't take her if she doesn't want to come."

"She's a lovely child," said Ruby.

"You mustn't let her looks persuade you."

Ruby meant lovely inside. She hadn't properly seen what Fleur looked like outside because Fleur's flower-fairy face had mostly been hidden inside her jersey.

"But we couldn't take her if she didn't want to come," said Rob. "It wouldn't be fair."

Miss Ream agreed. "But there's several other children who urgently need homes, if you're interested? We've got a very intelligent little girl of eight, who'd be much more rewarding in the long run. She plays Scrabble and chess and draws beautifully."

"No, thank you," said Rob.

And then, the door of Miss Ream's office opened slowly and Fleur came in. She was still hidden inside her jersey. She went over to where Rob and Ruby were sitting in front of Miss Ream's desk, dragging another chair with her, and she sat down beside them. Then she made a hole with her fingers through the knitting of the jersey and looked out at them.

"Hello, Fleur's Ruby," she said through the hole. "Hello, Fleur's Rob."

Miss Ream decided that perhaps it was worth taking a chance.

"You better come and look at our cottage," said Rob to Fleur. "We can't offer a lot, though we do the best we can."

Ruby said nothing.

Fleur sat in the pick-up truck between them, and looked out of the window at the passing houses, then the passing trees and fields till they arrived at the cottage on the farm. Ruby helped Fleur out and they went across the yard full of hens to the cottage door.

"This is Fleur," said Rob to Angela, David, Lizzie, Nevil, Jane, and Andrew who were sitting round the kitchen table eating bread and jam.

These children did not come and go and change like the children at Fairlawns Children's Home, but stayed all the time with Rob and Ruby and never went away, except to go to school but they always came back in time for tea. And the big ones helped look after the little ones. The little ones helped look after the hens, and the littlest one of all didn't do anything much except bang a wooden spoon on his chair.

After tea, Rob said to Fleur, "Fleur, would you like to stay here, like the others?" But he wasn't sure if Fleur understood for she said nothing, only went over to the scullery window and seemed to be watching the sun setting over the fields.

"At least she didn't say no," said Rob to Ruby.

Rob said to Fleur, "See that shed over there?"

Fleur nodded.

"There's a great tit's nest in a little crack in the wall of that shed. The hen tit laid seven tiny eggs on Sunday. She's sitting on them now, hatching them out."

"Birds," said Fleur for she could see some other birds on a tree.

"That's right," said Rob. "And them ones you can see is starlings."

Fleur saw the starlings, sitting in a line on the branch, dark birds with bright roving eyes and small heads.

Birds like Marilyn, she thought to herself. Not very pretty but not their fault.

"Marilyn like that," Fleur said to Rob.

Rob didn't know what she meant because he didn't know who Marilyn was, nor did he know about traveling on the school bus each day. But he could see Fleur meant something about the starlings, so he said, "Tomorrow we'll put them some bread out. For them starlings. And if you stay on, you'll see the blue tits hatch out and then their parents feeding them."

Later that evening after Fleur was tucked up in the small bed under the window in Lizzie, Jane and Angela's room, Rob walked down to the telephone kiosk at the crossroads and rang Miss Ream.

"Fleur's staying," he said. "Just for a bit."

Miss Ream said, "All right." And she sent a letter to the manager of the Special Schools Bus Service informing them that, for the time being, Fleur was to be collected from her new place, Rob and Ruby's cottage on the farm.

Fleur, waiting at the cottage door, holding Ruby's hand, watched the white mini-bus bumping towards them down the rough farm track. When it pulled up, Fleur walked over to the door and said to Bertram, the driver,

"This Fleur's Ruby-lady." She pointed to Ruby. Then she pointed away across the farm to where Rob was driving a herd of cows out to their pasture.

"Fleur's Rob-gentleman," she said.

"Well, I never did!" said Bertram. "Well, hop in then, love."

Fleur never said anything again. But she still lives with Rob and Ruby and sometimes, after Nevil and Jane have fed the hens, and Angela and Lizzie have bathed Andrew, and Jane and Ruby have cleared away the tea, and Fleur has put out the crusts and the crumbs for the starlings, Rob comes in from milking and sits by the window with Fleur and tells her this story.

6

GAIL'S BROTHER

I, Gail Russell, was five years old when my brother was born.

"Don't want a brother, thank you," I said when first shown the newborn in his crib.

"Hate babies," I said when first Thoby pursed up his delicate cherub lips at me in a lopsided grin of greeting.

"But look, he's smiling at you!" said the parents.

"Hate little boys," I said the first time the tiny pink hand clutched at my finger and created the unbreakable sibling bond.

"Gail, dear," said Mother, gently taking me onto her knee. "Why d'you always have to hate him when he loves you so much?"

"He's smelly and wet and horrid," I said. "And he can't *do* anything. What's the use of a person if it can't *do* anything?"

And so, those caring parents made sure that Baby Thoby was never wet or smelly, or at least not when I saw him.

"Boys are rough and rude and stupid," I said when Toddler Thoby first banged out pat-a-cake, pat-a-cake on the side of his cot with the palm of his fat little hand. But I lied, for Thoby was neither rough nor stupid. He was gentle and affectionate and it was I who was rude and stupid, and sometimes rather rough.

However, it was thanks to me that they discovered Thoby's wondrous talent. And it happened like this.

For eons and eons of time, I had been learning the piano. Despite the fact that there's not a drop of music in me, the parents thought I should learn. So, like an unwilling cart horse, I plodded through my *études*. But my wrists were wooden. My fingers were inflexible. Unmusically I fumbled for notes which never seemed to be in the right place.

As though dreary piano lessons weren't enough, the parents enrolled me to go each Wednesday after school to General Music class. The only good thing about this was that my best friend, Jen, went too. We sat together at the back, coloring in all the treble clefs into clowns' faces.

One Wednesday as Mother delivered me by car to the Music Center with my plastic recorder in its little cloth bag and my grubby sheets of staved paper, Thoby on the back seat began to clamor to be allowed to come too.

"Wanna go to music wiv her," he said. "Wanna do the music wiv my Gail!" He was four then.

"No, Thoby," said Mother. "Music is for big boys and girls. You and I are going to have a nice time going to the swings." She was always so anxious to protect me from him, living in the hope that, if carefully enough protected, I might eventually come to love him.

I said, as much to my own surprise as hers, "He might as well come with me, if he wants to so much." Nonchalantly, I added, "Won't make any difference to me if he's there or not."

"But he's so young. He'll only be a nuisance to you."

71

"There's other little ones. Jen's sister sometimes comes. She's only six."

Mother, overjoyed at what she saw as a first hopeful sign of bonding, relented.

"Very well. But listen, Thoby," she warned, patting the top of his darling silky head. "You must promise to be good as good as gold and not annoy kind big sister."

"Pwomiss, pwomiss," said Thoby as I roughly seized him by the arm and dragged him from the car and into the Center, quickly before Mother had time to change her mind. I was beginning to be interested in the prospect of bringing a real live brother to class. He would be my trophy, my distraction from the tedium of music theory.

And that afternoon, there beside me on the bench, Thoby's life in music began. Even gooder than gold, he sat through the session, transfixed by Miss Williams and her magic conductor's baton. By the end of that session he was beating out his rhythm on a drum, sorting his quavers from his demi-semi-quavers, more eagerly than ever I had done.

"Like it, Gail," he whispered as the lesson ended. "Like it lots and lots. Can I come next time again?"

So the following Wednesday he came with me once more. And soon after that, on the recommendation of the observant Miss Williams, he began piano lessons, then tuition on the half-size cello.

"Call that stringy rasping, music?" I said to Mother. "Sounds to me more like a rat crying in pain."

What was to me most curious and exciting was to see how much little Thoby seemed genuinely to enjoy it. There was no doubt about it. He was what the parents had wanted me to be. He was some kind of an infant prodigy.

Effortlessly he sailed through his recitals with commendations and distinctions. When he overtook me on piano, I gave that up, though to appease the parents, I ungraciously agreed to continue with the recorder, which I managed to play both breathily and squeakily.

"Hiya, old clever clogs! Oh, child of superior talent!" I said as I came in from school to find him already seated astride his mini-cello and trilling up and down his arpeggios.

To Mother, in the kitchen, I said, "He ought to be outside enjoying himself with a football like other boys his age."

Mother, pouring tea as though it were some kind of soothing balm for grazed feelings that Thoby, five years my junior, had so easily outshone me, said gently, "Gail dearest. Try not to be jealous of him. You're precious too, you know."

"Jealous? Me? What of? There's tons of kids at school who play just as well as that. He'll probably grow out of it by the time he's ten. It'll all just fizzle up into nothing."

Foolish unseeing Mother. How totally she misunderstood. There were no hurt feelings, no jealousy, only adoration and admiration.

"As a matter of fact," I went on, "I'm only too pleased that someone else in this family is prepared to slave away at their dreary scales for three hours a day."

That much was true. I *was* pleased. But never could I allow them to see how pleased and proud I was.

He didn't show off about his talent, for music was part of him, quite naturally, just as being bad-tempered and hostile to the parents seemed to be a part of me.

Sometimes when I was upstairs doing homework, I opened the bedroom door just a crack so I could listen to him practicing. Sometimes as I struggled to get my fingers to accomplish a tricky run of notes on the recorder, he would come and show me how. "Hey look, Gail, try it this way, like that, see." And when he showed me some new technique, he never said, "It's easy." He always knew that for me it was hard. It was only for him that it was easy.

It was from Thoby himself that I learned to accept people as they are, rather than for what they can do, which, when he later became as he did, made it possible for me to go on loving him just the same.

Thoby was eight, with his future in professional music already clearly mapped out when he had the accident which changed things so much, and in a curious kind of way, eventually made everything so much better between me and the parents.

It was my thirteenth birthday. Thoby had written a composition for me, his first ever piece. It was to be played to me during birthday tea.

"Now, darling," Mother announced, "Thoby's done something really nice for you."

"Done you some music, big sis," he said. "It's my pwesent." Even at eight, he still lisped like a younger child. "Hope you like it."

Thoby fetched in his cello and settled himself around it.

"In honor of Miss Gail Wussell," he solemnly said, "I wish to play *The Air and Vawiation on a Birthday Theme*, composed by the cellist."

Mother leaned across the table and hissed in my ear, "Gail dear, do try and look pleased even if you aren't. He's put a lot of effort into this."

Blind Mother. Why couldn't she ever see what I felt for him?

Thoby's music, the music which he had created, sounded to my ears as though it had been plucked from the wind, pulled out of the evening air. It flowed from his instrument like warm honey dripping from a spoon. It filled the room like sunshine.

I loved Thoby and his gift to me more than anybody in the world, more than Mother, more than Father, more than my best friend Jen. At that moment, on my thirteenth birthday, when his music stopped, I suddenly realized I loved him with an intensity which was overwhelming and inappropriate and nobody, least of all Thoby himself, would ever be able to love me back like this. I ran from the room in tears and confusion.

They gave me a bike for my birthday, a real flashy one. *Pink Princess Roadstar* it was called, with its bright rose and silvered frame, its pink and blue accessories. It had a rose-pink water bottle with a silver stripe down the side, like a racer's bike, attached in a special metal cradle to the frame. I imagined myself, miles from home, skimming along open roads on that wonderful machine, leaning down to take quenching sips of liquid from the stylish water bottle like some professional roadster.

It was a smarter present than anything I had been expecting and I guessed they were trying to demonstrate that they loved me too, even though I had no talent, even though I claimed less of their time and attention than my brilliant brother.

"You've only got me a bike to make up for the fact I'm stupid," I said.

"Of course you're not stupid, dear."

I was so ungracious that day.

Perhaps, with this amazing bike, they even thought to turn me into a sporting daughter, second-rate substitute for a musical one?

We were playing with it out in the garden. Not on the road, even I wasn't going to be allowed out on the road till Father had been with me to accustom me to traffic. They've always been such protective parents that it seems unjust any accident should have happened.

So it wasn't a case of neglect because we were all there, right near him. It should never have happened. But it did.

I was fooling around with the bike on the lawn while

75

Thoby sat up in the apple tree watching, admiring my antics. I was showing off to cover my embarrassment over the emotional outburst earlier on. Mother was gardening. Father was pottering in the shed. Both of them there. The whole happy little family at rest and play in their garden on the eldest child's thirteenth birthday.

Mother glanced up from her dahlias.

"Gail," she said. "I know it's your new present. But don't you think it might be a nice gesture to let Thoby have a turn?"

"It's too big for him," I said. "The seat's too high."

I knew because I'd already offered him a turn and he'd found he couldn't balance properly.

"I'll lower it for him," called Father from the shed and came out with a bike spanner.

"Go on, Thoby, Gail's offering you a turn. Isn't that nice?"

"S'all wight, mum," Thoby called down from his branch in the tree, "I've had a go. It's too big. Anyway, I don't weally like bikes. I like being in my twee best."

But Father had already loosened the bolt, lowered the saddle and tightened it all up again. They insisted Thoby come down from his tree and ride the bike, my bike, across the lawn.

They were always trying to engineer the relationship between us. Why couldn't they just let us get on with it ourselves?

He managed all right, wibble-wobble towards the concrete path where the front wheel caught the edge of the path and he went over the handlebars. Lots of boys fall head-first off bikes. Girls too. I've done it myself off my friend Jen's bike. I landed on my shoulder, which hurt so much that I couldn't do my piano practice properly. Mother thought I was just making excuses. It would've been all right for Thoby if only he'd landed on his shoulder. Or his ear. Or his elbow.

He landed on his head. Lots of lads land on their heads.

That would have been all right too if he'd been on the grass. The bike was on the grass. But Thoby's head wasn't on the grass.

It was on the concrete pillar that supports the fence between our garden and next door. It was like slow motion watching him go over the handlebars. He didn't cry out. He looked as though he were dead. Perhaps he was dead. We thought he was dead. I was sure he was dead because he didn't move, just lay quite still, not even much of a mark on him, just a bit of gray dust on his cheek from the dry earth in the flowerbed.

The kids from next door hung around our gate, watching the ambulance men unfold their stretcher. Later on I was sent next door to stay with them. Six o'clock was the worst. That's when I missed Thoby most. Six o'clock, always on the dot, was when Thoby did his cello practice. Every night. First the piano for twenty minutes. Then at six o'clock, he set up his music stand, opened up his case, and closed the sitting-room windows so as not to disturb the neighbors. Scales first, up and down like fish flying, then exercises like bells chiming. If I was upstairs in my room doing homework, that's when I'd open my door a crack to hear it wafting up the stairs. But now I was downstairs, next door, watching the six o'clock news with the neighbors and there was no music coming through the wall from my home on the other side. There was no Thoby because he was on a life support machine down at the hospital. After the panic, the waiting, the telephoning, the seeing if he'd live. The following day they moved him to another hospital that specializes in brains, miles away, so I didn't get to see what he looked like.

The next days were a blur of comings and goings. Mother cried a lot. Father didn't speak much. For them, it was as though he had actually died.

I stayed out of their way as much as I could. I never played again with the Princess bike, and after a while it got put right at the back of the shed. Eventually it disappeared altogether. I guess they gave it away. Ten days later on, they took me to the hospital sixty-seven miles away. I was really scared of going in to see him. I didn't quite know what I was expecting. He was at the end of the ward in a cot with iron sides as though he'd turned back into a baby. He seemed very small. But he looked all right. He had a plastic name-tag around his wrist and a tube up his nose and his eyes were shut.

Since he couldn't see or speak there didn't seem to me much point in visiting him. But they went anyway. They were waiting for consultants' diagnoses. Perhaps they were waiting for miracles too.

The next time I saw him he was off most of the machines. He could breathe by himself now. That was the limit of his skills. They'd taken X-rays of his skull, looking right inside to see what was going on in there. Not a lot.

He was as pale as a shadow. Otherwise much the same. But of course he wasn't the same. It was as if there was no one in there.

"It's almost as though there's no one in there, isn't it?" I said to Mother. She shook her head hopelessly, and rushed from the ward. The nurses were very kind but always distant.

When Father and I came out, Mother was sitting quietly in a rose-garden at the side of the hospital, composing herself.

That night, at home, I overheard Father describing the state of Thoby's brain to Uncle Matt on the phone.

Father sounded angry and upset. "Take one whole cooked cauliflower," he shouted down the line as though the accident were Uncle Matt's fault. "Hit it once with a sledgehammer and what do you get? Gray pulp, that's what! That's our Thoby's brain!"

Then Father cried instead and Mother had to go to the telephone and finish the call.

They thought he might be blind as well. No one could be sure.

We went twice a week after school, sixty-seven miles there, sixty-seven miles back. I couldn't bear it with just the two of them, sitting by the cot, always one or the other of them crying. And nothing to do but sit there.

I told Jen about it during break. I told Jen quite a lot these days.

"He's probably going to be a sort of vegetable," I said. "That's what they say." With a brain like a smashed-up cauliflower, he wasn't going to be playing Schubert's String Quintet in C, that was for sure.

"You could try singing," Jen said. "To pass the time."

"Singing? How d'you mean?"

"He might like it, and if they're both wailing they won't notice."

"You know I can't sing for toffee," I said. "Anyway, I'd look a right dumbhead singing to a person who can't think."

"Not half as daft as he must look, lying there with a tube stuck up his poor little nose."

"He's off being fed with tubes. The nurses are trying to teach him to swallow by himself."

On visiting day I discovered that he probably wasn't blind. I was leaning over the side of his cot idly dangling a piece of string onto his face to see if he'd twitch his nose, when he suddenly seemed to look at me, quite definitely look. Of course, he's looking all the time, staring ahead in a vacant way. But it wasn't that. It was a *real* look. His eyes touched mine, and for a couple of seconds they seemed to hold on, before drifting back into their own world. I flicked him with the piece of string again but to no effect.

Then I realized it wasn't the string. It was the humming. I'd been humming, in my own tuneless sort of way, *She'll be Coming Round the Mountain When She Comes*.

I was so excited I could hardly contain myself.

On the next visit three days later, I took my recorder with me and I was alone with Thoby. The parents had been summoned to an interview with the consultant neurologist.

I took it out of its cloth bag and I stood close by Thoby's cot and I put the mouthpiece to my lips. I blew a C, and a D, and an E. Then I began to play the first tune that came into my head. It was *Greensleeves*, the best of a bad bunch. But for once I really tried my best to get it right.

Thoby blinked, so I went on. But I'd only done the first two and a half bars when one of the nurses came hurrying over the shiny linoleum floor.

"Sssh dear, not here!" she said, putting her finger to her lips. My playing wasn't *that* bad. Besides, there was already the sound of one child in his crib moaning quietly, the rattle of plates on a trolley, and the television perched up on a shelf blaring away.

"Some of these little children are very sick, you know. You mustn't upset them."

She was only young. Another nurse, higher up the hierarchy, in a different colored uniform, a differently shaped cap, and more badges pinned to her apron front, came over and said,

"That's all right dear. So long as none of the little ones are trying to sleep, you play your brother a nice nursery rhyme."

Nice nursery rhyme! Didn't she know that *Greensleeves* was composed by Henry VIII?

"And you never know, he might even be listening."

Might be! Of *course* he was listening. He couldn't tell me but I could see it in his eyes that he was listening. And twitching.

Let the music go into your ears, your head, into your neck, your shoulders, your tummy, your toes. Let your head dance, little boy, your eyes dance, your fingers dance.

I started *Greensleeves* from the beginning again and played it through twice. It was slightly better the final time round, hardly brilliant, but if you already happened to know the tune, you'd have got it.

Thoby got it. His head moved, quite definitely. I was so excited I was almost twitching myself.

"O.K., little man," I said. "So what d'you want next?"

Since he couldn't reply, it was a mere formality asking. In fact, he had no choice. He had to have whatever was in my limited repertoire.

I managed another run through of *Greensleeves* with no slips, then *The Rose of the South.*

The parents returned to the ward.

"Look, I'm sure, quite sure he hears something!" I said. "He still likes music."

But they were too wrapped up in the new phase of their pain to be interested in the achievements of my cheap plastic recorder. The neurologist had spoken. There were to be no miracles. There was irreversible brain damage to the outer cells of the cortex, affecting motor and thought processes, also sensory perception.

The sixty-seven-mile drive home was terrible that night. They had to decide whether to bring him home, or find him a place in a long-stay hospital for vegetables. I thought to myself, If they put him away, I'll leave.

I said, to break the awfulness, "It's not that bad."

Neither of them in the front said anything.

I said, "I mean, at least he's still *alive*. And he can hear.

He smiled at me. You saw it. Surely you saw it? I'm going to play to him, and play to him, and get him better."

Mother said, "You've always been jealous, haven't you, Gail? Ever since he was little."

She didn't understand.

She said, "Sometimes I think you're glad this has happened."

I was glad because he had listened to my music just as I used to listen to his and liked it. That was what I was glad about.

"It's nothing to do with anyone being jealous," I said. "We've got to live with him like he is now, not like he *might* have been."

At last they brought him home. He seemed to have stuck at four and a half months old. He dribbled a bit, but he smiled too, and sometimes waved his hands about as though conducting an invisible and silent orchestra. The parents sat him on the settee in the front room, propped up with cushions. He didn't seem to know he'd come home. He didn't recognize any of it, which was a pity. But at least he was back with us. I knew I was going to love him. I snuggled up beside him and sang *Yankee Doodle's Gone to Town* as I counted his fingers.

Mother said, "What's going to be the purpose in his life now?"

I felt sad for her because she was so upset. But I didn't feel sad for Thoby. He was still himself. I wished she could see that.

Mother said, "It's all very well, Gail, at the moment while he's little and cute. But what about later when he grows up?"

"What about it?"

"When your father and I aren't around anymore."

Why won't she come to the point?

"You mean, when you're both dead?"

"We can't expect you to take care of him when you're grown-up, now can we?"

"Why not?"

"What if you get married?"

I just laughed. "At my age, Mother, for goodness sake? You want me to start thinking about marriage already?"

Now he was home I wanted Jen to come in and see him. At first, she wouldn't. "I'm ever so squeamish about things like that, Gail," she said.

"Please," I said. After all, it was her who'd first had the good idea about singing to him. In the end I persuaded her, though I know she didn't really want to.

"Just for a moment," I said. "Just to say hello."

"I thought you said he couldn't talk?"

He was in his usual place, propped up with cushions like a little prince. He appeared not to see her. He often doesn't seem to be seeing people, and then afterwards when you mention their names, he gets excited and you realize he has known they were there.

"Hey Jen, you want to see what happens when he hears singing?" I said.

Jen did. We both sang a song we learned once in General Music, *Shalom, Shalom! Hallo, hallo!* After a few moments, Thoby's mouth flickered with a smile and he began to shake his head up and down and round and round. He *was* listening. When we'd finished he reached his hand out towards Jen as though to touch her. She looked dead scared, but then she suddenly put her arms round him, dribble and all, and hugged him.

"He's lovely," she said after. "Really sweet. You know, Gail, I never thought I could touch a dummy person and not mind. But he's just like normal really, isn't he?"

After that, she came nearly every day, and so did other

people. For people who didn't know, it was just a question of getting used to him. Gradually Thoby began to learn to do things. Lately, he's even begun trying to feed himself. I saw him pick up a dead fly lying on the windowsill and put it in his mouth. He didn't look as though he liked the taste much but at least it's a start. Soon, he's going to start going to a special kind of school for kids like him. They'll send a bus for him every morning.

When he first had the accident it was as though our family had been completely broken up, like a perfect china jug being smashed to bits on a stone floor. Now the jug has been put together again. You can still see the joins and cracks and glue but they don't matter. In fact, because of those cracks we're an even better, more interesting jug than we were before.

Of course there are times when I feel sad about Thoby, days when nothing seems to happen to him, when he doesn't change at all, evenings when I know the parents are exhausted by looking after him and I wonder what the point is.

But there are more of the other kind of days when I am so strong and capable and I come running all the way home from the bus stop because I can't wait to get to see him.

On those days, it's all worth it. Thoby's tiny smiles are more valuable than most people's.

7

DANNY

*D*anny and his Aunty Beth lived in their basement flat underneath Mrs. Jalabhay's house. They didn't have much money. But they had a lot of fun. When it was rainy, they ate toast and honey by their fire and made music with the saucepans. When it was gloomy, they made toffee and painted pictures on the kitchen door. When it was sunny they went to the park and lay under the trees singing. When it was snowy, they went to the park and slid down the slope on a tin tray.

Every fortnight Danny went with Aunty Beth to cash her welfare check at the post office. Then they went home and put two buns and a piece of cheese in a carrier bag for their dinner, and they walked to the bus stop, and waited for a bus to come along.

"Which bus today?" said Danny, waving his arms through the air like a flying bus. "Which bus today? Hurray, hurray. Bus comes today."

Every week they got on a different bus and went to find some fun at a different place.

"Where to, duckie?" the bus conductor would ask.

"Anywhere you're going," said Aunty Beth.

"We don't mind. We don't mind," said Danny. "We're going venturing to find the fun."

Aunty Beth once told Danny that if you stayed on a bus, any bus, for long enough, you always ended up somewhere interesting and found some fun.

"Well I'll be blowed!" said the conductor. "That's a darn funny way of going on a bus."

"Danny and me are darn funny people," said Aunty Beth. "But we try to serve the Lord with gladness."

Sometimes they went in one direction, sometimes in another. They went to the market, and to the hospital. They went to the railway station to look at the trains arriving and departing. They went to the docks to see the ships unloading. Once, they went to the safari park to watch the people watching the monkeys.

If it was raining, they stayed on the bus until it reached the end of its trip and turned round and started back again.

Aunty Beth knew that Danny was different from other children in lots of ways. She knew, for instance, that he needed to learn things in a different way from how Mrs. Jalabhay's daughter upstairs learned. Aysha Jalabhay learned things from books and from doing hours and hours of homework.

"You need to learn things by doing," said Aunty Beth.

"And buses," said Danny. "Lot of buses."

Danny's favorite bus was the one that said it went to a place called World's End, for Aunty Beth had once told him a wonderful story about when the world would end and the sky would be scarlet, and there would be lots of people out in the streets, and goats and sheep running everywhere.

"And then shall we understand," said Aunty Beth, "how the foolishness of God is wiser than men."

Danny couldn't read the names on the front of the buses,

but Aunty Beth always told him what they said. She showed him how the buses had numbers on the front too.

Aunty Beth said, "It's not going to the end of the world. It's only the name of a pub at the end of the route. I once went there on a mission long ago. When I was younger than what I am now."

Even when Aunty Beth told him World's End was only the name for a pub, Danny still liked the sound of it and he hoped that one day they'd get on the right bus to go there.

"Well, there's lots of places with the same name," said Aunty Beth. "But there is only one place that is known by many names. And that's the Heavenly Kingdom."

Aunty Beth had looked after Danny for a long time. They'd had lots of fun together. And she'd showed him plenty of useful things, like how to get his socks on so the heels were comfy on his heels, and how to get each of his shoes on the proper foot, and how to pour a drink without slopping on the floor. She'd taught him always to watch her face when she talked. She'd taught him to listen, to watch, to sing and to clap his hands in time to music.

"The good Lord may not have given you much in the way of wisdom. But your eyes are His gift. So you jolly well use them."

Aunty Beth loved Danny very much. And Danny liked living with her in the basement flat because when you weren't going out on buses, you could sit by the window and watch people's feet as they walked past on the pavement above.

One welfare check day Aunty Beth and Danny were just getting themselves sorted out to set off on an adventure when a person in a brown coat came to call at the basement flat. They saw her feet in brown shoes coming down the steps first.

Danny went to the door.

"Just going out," he said to the person in the brown coat with the big brown feet.

But the person came in anyway. "It's Miss Kipling I've come to see," she said.

Danny didn't know who Miss Kipling was.

"Oh, dearie me!" said the person in the brown coat, looking round the basement flat. "Have I caught you rather on the hop, Miss Kipling?"

She seemed to think that Aunty Beth was Miss Kipling and that Miss Kipling's flat was in a bit of a mess.

"Nice mess," thought Danny.

He and Aunty Beth had had one of their painting days. Aunty Beth had painted some of the floor to look like a checkerboard. Danny had painted his socks a bit too.

"I dare say, Miss Kipling, you were just about to get down to your housework? So I won't keep you for too long," said the person in the brown coat.

"No," said Danny. "Crematorium."

"Excuse me?" said Mrs. Brown Coat.

"We're just on our way out," said Aunty Beth. "I take the laddie out once a fortnight on educational trips. We're off down to the Crematorium. We went to St. Paul's the other week, caught the tail end of a funeral. So I thought it'd make proper sense of it to visit where the burnings are, just so he knows."

"Dead people rising up," Danny explained. "Bus number 546."

Danny couldn't always speak clearly, or read words, but he was getting better at remembering figures. Aunty Beth was teaching him to count money too.

Mrs. Brown Coat wouldn't sit down, and she wouldn't accept a cup of tea. And Danny could see that she upset Aunty Beth rather a lot.

"I am the school welfare officer, Miss Kipling," she said.

"And I'm afraid I've had to come and remind you once again that the boy must start attending."

"Oh botheration. School, school, school," said Aunty Beth crossly. "What good would school do a chappie like him? He's learning plenty more with me. We go out on the buses and see lots. Just so long as he learns to honor all men and fear the Lord, he'll be all right in this life, and maybe even the next."

"Maybe. But the law's the law. According to the 1981 Education Act, all children regardless of ability are obliged to attend. And it's high time you took notice of the fact, Miss Kipling, or you're likely to find yourself in big trouble. A place has been waiting for the boy ever since you moved into the area and you know it."

Aunty Beth said, "I'm not sure he'd be happy in a big school. The children would tease him. Clever children can be very cruel, you know. And I don't want nobody making fun of him with their vipers' tongues."

Danny listened, carefully watching her face, and wondered what she meant. Nobody had ever made fun of him. He wished they would. Fun was good. Fun was what he did with his Aunty Beth, once a fortnight when she got her money.

He waved his arms round like branches on a tree in a wind.

"Integration is the policy in this area," said the visitor as she buttoned her coat. "For statemented and non-statemented children."

Danny didn't know what that meant. Nor did Aunty Beth.

"But where shall wisdom be found and where is the place of understanding?" she muttered under her breath.

"Miss Kipling, if he doesn't start learning soon, he'll fall even more behind."

"It's not school learning what's important for boys like him," said Aunty Beth. "It's being."

Mrs. Brown Coat picked up her bag. "You'll be hearing from me."

Danny hopped over to the window to watch Mrs. Brown Coat going up the steps to ground level above.

"Don't like that person," he said, to show solidarity with Aunty Beth who loved him most in all the world. But all the same, he wondered what school was like, specially if there was good fun to be had there.

"Well maybe it wouldn't do you too much harm to find out," said Aunty Beth.

"Like World's End?" Danny wondered. He often thought about World's End.

"Not much," said Aunty Beth.

So Aunty Beth got Danny ready for going to school with two buns and a piece of cheese in a bag, just like going on a bus.

Danny felt proud to be walking along the road with Aunty Beth and a special bag made out of a pillowcase for his shoes. Aunty Beth pointed out interesting things on the way for Danny to look at and remember, so he'd be able to find his own way home. He already knew the telephone kiosk on the corner, and the post office where Aunty Beth cashed her welfare check, and the baker where they bought the buns.

To begin with, Danny liked school. He liked watching the other children play on the climbing frame, he liked the dinners, he liked the big picture on the classroom wall of a field full of woolly sheep grazing in a faraway place. He wondered if it was World's End. But when he climbed up onto the shelves to get nearer to the faces of the sheep to hear them speak to him, the teacher shouted. Danny didn't bother to listen to her shouting, but he knew from her face.

There was another part of school which Danny didn't

like. It was when the Reading Mum came. She was Jenny's mum.

"Jenny's a great little reader," said the Reading Mum. "Let's see if our new boy can be a great little reader too."

The Reading Mum came in to help the teacher help the children. Danny liked being helped by his Aunty Beth to do things which were difficult. But the Reading Mum wasn't a bit like Aunty Beth. She didn't smile very often, except at her own Jenny. She was more like Mrs. Brown Coat.

"Look, dear," she said. "D for Danny. D. D. D. And do try and control your arms, can't you?"

"Going home," said Danny. "Going home. World's End."

"*Surely* you can see the D? *Everybody* knows their own name."

"Yes," said Danny.

Of course Danny knew his own name. The Reading Mum wanted him to know the look of the D for Danny as well, so to please her he learned the D for Danny, and the A for An and the N for the end. And when he wrote them down like the Reading Mum told him to, he found he could make different patterns.

D was like a house in the night with a thousand lighted windows, A was an orange on a tree at World's End, N was the waves of the shiny sea. But it didn't make the Reading Mum pleased.

"Yes, dear. It's very pretty but it's not writing. They always have to be the same way and in the same order to be writing."

Danny wished he could be at home making saucepan music and toffee with Aunty Beth. He wished he could be on a bus with Aunty Beth.

Most days, Danny came home on his own, for Aunty Beth was still at work. She went to clean people's offices. Danny used to go with her and sit quietly doing nothing till Aunty Beth had finished the job. Now he went to school while she was at work.

"What's he saying now?" said the Reading Mum. "I can't make out a word that boy says."

Danny crawled under the table and made a noise like a monkey in a safari park and some of the other children came over and stared at him. Jenny giggled.

"The new boy's a spazzy," she said.

By the time school was over that day, the rest of the children were calling out "Spazzy Spazzy" too.

Danny laughed, and joined in, and waved his arms like paper kite-tails flying high in the air. When he got home, he told his Aunty Beth what he had learned.

"What's that, you're saying?"

"Spizzy spazzy!" said Danny.

Aunty Beth wasn't pleased. "Don't you use that kind of language round here," she said sharply. "Where d'you pick up that kind of talk?"

Danny didn't mind them calling him Spazzy, but he did mind about the letters. He worried and worried about the shape of them. They seemed to go round and round in front of his eyes, but he couldn't put them in the right order like the Reading Mum wanted.

Danny wondered if Aunty Beth was lonely all day without him.

"Well, I do miss you, Danny," Aunty Beth told him. "But I try to remember the patience of Job. Besides, I know I'll see you again in the afternoon, as soon as I'm back from work."

After their tea, they made music together and Danny forgot about worrying. Then they played dominoes. Then they played Snap. Next they told each other stories. Aunty Beth told Danny a story about a bush which caught on fire. Danny told a story about a boy and an old aunty who lived in a basement flat. Aunty Beth could nearly always understand what Danny was saying even when other people couldn't.

Finally, Aunty Beth gave Danny a wash at the sink and tucked him up in his bed with a hot water bottle, for it can sometimes be damp and chilly living in a basement. Then she settled down with her knitting. Danny felt safe in bed.

But when there was a knock at the door and Mrs. Brown Coat came into the flat, Danny didn't feel so cozy any more. He watched her through a crack in his door. Had she come to take him to school again?

He heard her say to his Aunty Beth how no child should be left on his own in the basement. "And specially not a child like that."

"There's Mrs. Jalabhay upstairs," said Aunty Beth. "She's always there if he needs anything before I'm back. She's always been understanding with Danny. She may worship a heathen god at another temple, but I'm telling you, some of these Asians understand a lot better than us about caring for the weaker lambs in the flock."

Danny remembered Mrs. Jalabhay bringing down a plate of poppadums on his birthday. And there'd been jellabys at Christmas.

Mrs. Brown Coat said, "He shouldn't be walking home on his own, either."

Aunty Beth said, "He's plenty old enough."

"Is he *able* enough, that's the problem? He's been seen wandering out on the road. What if something happens to him on his way home?"

Danny thought how several good things had happened to him coming home. He'd jumped in a puddle, rolled in some dry leaves and walked along the top of a high scary wall.

"What if? What if? What if?" said Aunty Beth. "What if

the Day of Judgement is tomorrow? Anyway, from what I've heard, he'll come to more harm from teasing in that classroom of his than what he will out on the street."

When Mrs. Brown Coat went Aunty Beth began to cry. Danny couldn't remember seeing her cry before.

He got out of bed and fetched her a piece of paper from the dark toilet along the passage where there were sometimes centipedes.

"Blow!" he said. "Blow, blow, like the mighty rushing breeze."

That's what she used to say to him to teach him to blow his nose.

Aunty Beth blew. "Ah, that's better!" she said.

Danny fetched her a drink of juice, pouring it out without spilling any. Then he danced her a funny dance, and drew her a funny picture.

Danny wondered why she had been crying. "Why, why, why?" he said. "What happening?"

"Because if they don't think you're being properly looked after when you get home from school, they'll take you away."

"Can't do that," said Danny. "Can't." And he wondered if they could and he grew frightened. He had lived with Aunty Beth as long as he could remember, since he was born, perhaps even since before he was born, since the beginning of the world. If he didn't live with Aunty Beth, it would be the end of the world.

Danny wondered if it was to do with the letters? If he didn't learn the shapes of the letters, might they take him away from Aunty Beth forever?

"The letters," he said.

"What letters is that, duckie?" said Aunty Beth.

But Danny didn't know how to say.

"They say you're not getting on. But where do they want

94

you to get on to? I don't know about all this reading and stuff. Tell you the truth, I was never too good on that side myself. But you know, pet, I think maybe that welfare woman's got some sense. See, I can't teach you *all* the things you'll need to know after I've crossed over to the other side."

Danny wondered what other things he needed to know. Already, since starting school, he knew a lot. He knew the word to describe the color of Maggie's hair ribbons, and where Harry's scarf had been hidden, and how to keep very very quiet when he didn't want anybody to annoy him. But he couldn't say any of it so people would understand.

The other children knew how to talk, talk, talk all the time, about everything. They all had so many different words. And specially, they talked about spazzys, and divvys, and veggys, and spams and mongs, and joeys and fliddies and dappy-doos. Sometimes it seemed as if Aunty Beth was the only person in the world who remembered that his name was Danny.

Aunty Beth tried to look after Danny the way that Mrs. Brown Coat seemed to want, coming home early from her cleaning job, and looking after Danny when he wasn't at home by tidying the basement every day, and moving things about, so neither of them could find them when they wanted them.

Aunty Beth even tried to do something about the letters, tried to make learning letters feel like fun, like she'd made learning to do up buttons and shoelaces fun. She made a paper book for the learning. She made Danny write the name of the book on the outside. *Danny's Book* she wanted it to say.

"My book," Danny agreed, but when he wrote it, it didn't look right to Aunty Beth. It said koobs soobk kbooks kosob ksobo the AndDanny Koobs and NadnyDanny nadthe Kosob Bok.

Danny gave up trying to get the letters in the right order. Aunty Beth gave up.

"Don't reading," said Danny. "Other things."

Aunty Beth said she didn't mind about reading, she only minded about the teacher minding.

"Whatever am I to do about you?" she said and went along to the school to talk to the people there.

"Daniel is a spazmoid!" sang Jenny in the cloakroom.

"Daniel is more of a problem child than we anticipated," said his teacher.

"Oh, dear," said Aunty Beth. "He never has been before."

"He's a pest," said the dinner ladies to Aunty Beth. To Danny, they said, "Yes, you Daniel. You're a pest."

"He's getting worse," said the Reading Mum. "You're getting worse, Daniel."

"Not. Not, not," said Danny. "You spazzy, you dumbo."

"Not stay, not stay!" said Danny to himself, but he didn't say it loud enough for any of them to hear him, nor clear enough for anybody to understand him.

"World's End," he said. "On the bus. Praise the Lord in the beauty of holiness."

Danny walked slowly and quietly out of the school and when he was beyond the playground, he began to run, waving his arms like eagles flying over mountains. He ran far. He had to get away from the Reading Mum, from the letters that made the wrong patterns, from the noisy children teasing. He wanted to run away and find a bus to World's End. But without his Aunty Beth, he didn't know how to find the way.

He sat on a wall and waited. He wanted his Aunty Beth.

He waved his arms to the sky where eagles can fly. He knew the sky was too big for him without his Aunty Beth.

"Too big, the sky," he called.

So when he'd sat on the wall for long enough, he found his way back to the basement flat. He didn't want his Aunty Beth to be worrying about him either.

Mrs. Brown Coat was there too, sitting at the table drinking a cup of tea with Aunty Beth.

"So you see, Miss Kipling," she was saying, "we're varying our policy of integration over this one."

Aunty Beth didn't seem to see, but she was nodding politely to Mrs. Brown Coat.

"And we'd like to move him to a learning environment where he can really flourish, where we can offer him a structured learning program, exactly to suit his special needs."

"So you won't be taking him away from me?" said Aunty Beth.

"Oh goodness me, no! Not after all you've done for him. You've got him for life."

After Mrs. Brown Coat had had her long chat and gone away, Aunty Beth made Danny his tea and explained what was going to happen.

"You'll be going on a bus!" said Aunty Beth. "Every day. You'll enjoy that, won't you?"

"Bus!" said Danny, pleased and interested. "World's End?"

"No, not to World's End. To a different school, a special school which is better for you."

Danny wasn't so sure about that. He'd tried school.

"You may not like it all the time. But we can't always do exactly what we like, can we, Danny? Life is like a long journey as we travel towards the New Jerusalem. For here we have no continuing city but we seek one to come. And when at last we meet the All-Merciful, we'll enter into his courts with songs of joy and thanksgiving on our lips. And this new place you're going to is like another bit of your journey. And there'll be some good things there too. Painting. And singing. And growing things. That's what the welfare woman says."

So Aunty Beth got Danny ready for his new school.

Even though he was going to go on a bus, they didn't walk to a bus stop. Instead, the bus would come to collect Danny right from his home. When it arrived, Danny down in the basement saw the big tires drawing up against the curb. Aunty Beth took him up the steps to the pavement.

The driver of the bus got out to meet Danny. He shook him by the hand.

"Hello there, Danny," he said. He already knew Danny's name. That was good. "Welcome on board. Nice to have you join the crew."

A lady on the bus smiled and showed Danny to a seat.

Danny sat down and looked around. There were other children on the bus. It is always good to be with other people, if they are kind people.

"Good to be together," said Danny, clapping his hands together as Aunty Beth had taught him.

The boy sitting just in front of Danny turned round and smiled.

"Hello," he said. "Hello, my name's Jonathan. We'll be friends."

8

BERTRAM
IN THE AFTERNOON

At the end of his working day, Bertram drove the
empty bus into the garage, to park it in its bay.
Time to knock off, get home to his missus, take a squint
at the *Gazette*.

"And a rum old day it has been too," thought Bertram.
He checked on the cigarette saved behind his ear, then took
the logbook from its shelf under the dashboard to enter the
routine record of the day's events.

*"Morning journey without incident. On afternoon run,
3:17 p.m. light drizzle falling. Windscreen wipers ceased
functioning.*

"Funny that was," Bertram thought. "Them not working
all of a sudden. Must be a loose screw somewhere in there.
They was all right yesterday. Better get Bill to give all the
electrics a check-over first thing.

"3:18 p.m. Andrew Bright was took with seizure.

"Andy. Our little king of the road. Now why should he
go and do a thing like that? Hasn't had one in months.
And that wasn't your petit mal neither. It was your grand
mal, poor little fellow. Take him a day or so to get over
that. So that's Andy won't be with us tomorrow morning,
I dare say. We'll miss him on the run.

"Then, only a moment or two later, before I'd half realized what was going on between Andy and Mrs. Lovegrove in the back of the bus, all of a sudden there was this noise. Like an explosion it was. And straight after, I've got no control over where we're heading. Glad to say, there wasn't nothing about, not at that moment anyhow. Not like sometimes when you get these daft weirdos coming up behind you, headlamps flashing, trying to do a ton. Kamikaze morons I call them.

"Steering that bus was like the steering wheel had turned to rubber under my very hands and there we was careering all over the road like a mad dog." Bertram bit the end of the pencil while he wondered how to put this into appropriate language for the logbook.

"Proceeding at approximately 40 miles per hour along dual carriageway westward from city center, some 12 1/2 miles outside city boundary, forward offside tire punctured, causing vehicle to momentarily go into skid situation.

"Fortunate to relate," thought Bertram. "I know a skid the minute I'm into one. I wasn't no supplies driver with the Territorials for nothing. Steer with the skid, that's what you have to do. Like life. If you see life coming on at you, don't try and duck out the way or you'll land in more trouble still. Head right into it and like as not you'll know what you're tackling.

"Managed to regain control, held steady course, proceeded at decreasing speed towards curbside. Came to rest in ditch.

"All my little ones were firmly strapped in," Bertram congratulated himself. "Mrs. L. always makes sure of that. So no harm done."

In fact, it seemed they'd really rather enjoyed the unexpected excitement of being tipped into a ditch. Micky had immediately begun to rock happily from side to side in his place and to roar triumphantly. Rebecca had clapped her hands and cried, "More, Bertram! More more. We're going funfair!" Even Fleur had been laughing.

While Mrs. Lovegrove was busy attending to little Andy, Bertram hopped out to see what the damage was.

"Ripped to shreds, it was. Looked just like seaweed. Must've been something nasty on the road. First time in thirty years I've had a blow-out quite like that."

What came next had been all of a rush, before Bertram had time to so much as sneeze. Yet now, in recollecting it, it seemed as though it happened perfectly calmly and normally, no panic, no unruly behavior.

"It was our Marilyn at the back. Always been a bit of a sour little moppet. Bitter parents, that's the sadness. She used to be a runner-awayer when she was little. The gold medalist sprinter, we called her, Mrs. L. and I because she was never in one place for more than a minute. Well, she grew out of that, glad to recall, thanks to careful handling from Mrs. L. Or we thought she had. Come to think of it, maybe she wasn't running away at all. Just wanted to go and talk to the sheep?"

Bertram had just been straightening himself up from making his inspection of the tattered tire, when he saw gawky Marilyn with her handbag, not inside the bus but prancing about on the side of the road.

"How she ever got her seat belt undone, I'm sure I'll never know, let alone them rear doors. Them's all child-proof locks. Not as daft as she looks, our Marilyn, I dare say. Out the bus she was and skipping around in the wet grass with daisies in her hair. Just as though she were the Queen of the May. And blow me down if young Jonathan, usually as timid as a mouse, wasn't with her too.

"Then Rebecca leans out of the bus and starts yelling at me something ever so important. What was it she was on about this time? Always got something to say, our Rebecca. Well, it must've been them sheep she was trying to talk to me about. Because, next thing, there they all was, dozens of them beside the road, bleating away on the wrong side of the fence. How in blazes did they get there? Then Daniel's got himself out of the bus as well, and handing round chocolate biscuits, or so he says. Invisible biscuits of course. And our Micky begins singing his heart out. *Ain't Misbehaving* sounded like to me, though where'd he learn a tune like that? Well, I wasn't born yesterday. I knew there wasn't nothing much I could do till the back-up bus arrived. So there was nothing for it really. If you can't beat them, you have to join them. There we all was, sitting in the rain eating our biscuits what you couldn't see and couldn't taste, and talking to them sheep what wouldn't answer. And even Andy perked up enough for us to bring him out to join in the singsong. Got a lovely memory for songs, has Mrs. L."

Bertram, sitting in the parking bay, took the cigarette from behind his ear and fingered it absently. How to put all this into words, that was the difficulty. There wasn't room in the log book to write more than half a dozen lines for each day's record. He could overspill into the following day's entry of course, and hope not too much happened tomorrow. Or he could fetch an extra piece of paper from the office and stick it in.

Bertram lit the cigarette and thought carefully for a few moments. Then, with the rubber tip of his stub of pencil, he carefully erased his previous account of the day's events. Instead he wrote:

"Slight mechanical failure on homeward journey. Mrs. Lovegrove coped splendidly throughout. Passengers, as usual, magnificent. Otherwise, a normal day."

Bertram closed the log book and put it away till tomorrow.